'F
down *IFI Fantasy Guide*

D0550929

The Covenant series:

'Oh my Gods! Wow! Jennifer L. Armentrout is such an amazing writer; my heart is still beating hard against my rib cage' *Book Gossips*

'I am completely hooked on Jennifer Armentrout's Covenant series' *Love is Not a Triangle*

'A great blend of action, drama, and romance . . . simply amazing from beginning to end' *The Reading Geek*

'All the romance anyone would ask for, plus a whole lot of action and suspenseful drama as well' *The Revolving Bookcase*

'Ramps up the action, drama and suspense without ever losing a step' *Dreams in Tandem*

Jennifer L. Armentrout lives in West Virginia. All the rumors you've heard about her state aren't true. Well, mostly. When she's not hard at work writing, she spends her time reading, working out, watching zombie movies, and pretending to write. She shares her home with her husband, his K-9 partner named Diesel, and her hyper Jack Russell Loki. Her dreams of becoming an author started in algebra class, where she spent her time writing short stories . . . therefore explaining her dismal grades in math. Jennifer writes Adult and Young Adult Urban Fantasy and Romance.

Find out more at www.jenniferarmentrout.com
Follow her on Twitter@JLArmentrout
or find her on
Facebook/JenniferLArmentrout

JENNIFER L. ARMENTROUT

Tempting the Bodyguard

A Gamble Brothers Novel

HODDER

Tempting the Bodyguard first published in eBook in the United States of America in 2015 by Entangled Publishing, LLC

This paperback edition first published in Great Britain in 2015
by Hodder & Stoughton
An Hachette UK company

1

A CIP catalogue record for this title is available from the British Library

Paperback ISBN 978 1 473 61595 3
eBook ISBN 978 1 444 79853 1

Typeset by Hewer Text UK Ltd, Edinburgh
Printed and bound by Clays Ltd, St Ives plc

Hodder & Stoughton policy is to use papers that are natural, renewable
and recyclable products and made from wood grown in sustainable forests.
The logging and manufacturing processes are expected to conform
to the environmental regulations of the country of origin.

Hodder & Stoughton Ltd
Carmelite House
50 Victoria Embankment
London
EC4Y 0DZ

www.hodder.co.uk

Chapter One

Spread across the recently polished coffee table, twenty letters were open and faceup. The faint smell of lemon lingered in the air, a scent that reminded Alana Gore of her grandmother's house. Granny Gore had been obsessed with Pine-Sol like it was a geriatric version of crack cocaine. Everything, including the hardwood floors, had been doused in the stuff. As a small child, Alana had spent many of her afternoons after school using the hallway downstairs in the quiet home as a Slip'N Slide.

Granny had always kept everything neat and clean, to the point that it was borderline disturbing, which explained why Alana, as an adult, couldn't stand things to be displaced or messy. Everything had to be in order and have a purpose.

And what was resting on her coffee table definitely was not a part of the plan—of any plan.

Alana took a deep breath and let it out slowly. "Well, shit on a shitter."

Granny rolled over in her grave.

Cursing was unladylike, and while Alana strived to maintain a sensible, responsible image, in private, she cursed like a street thug in the middle of a drug deal gone baaaad. A habit she'd picked up in high school and hadn't been able to break since.

She leaned forward and picked up the most recent letter, the one that had arrived in the mail today—the one she had been dreading since February.

After working to repair the notorious reputation—which she had done so *spectacularly*, like always—of Chad Gamble, all-star pitcher for the Nationals, she'd decided to stay in Washington, D.C. There was something about the nation's capital that had drawn her in, and she really hadn't put roots down in L.A., not the kind that had her yearning to return home while traveling for work. All she had there was a small condo, and besides, she'd wanted out of the city for other reasons.

Like the letters lying on her table.

In her mind, moving to D.C. should've stopped this, because who would've seriously put effort into finding her clear across the country, in a different time zone? Someone who was absolutely psychotic.

And, well, that was problematic.

Smoothing the stray hairs at her temples, she cursed again. A nice, juicy little F-bomb. Her hands were *not* shaking. She was fine. They were just stupid letters from someone who was obviously on the deranged side of things. Letters couldn't hurt people.

But these letters . . .

Alana picked up the newest one, her lips compressing into a tight, tense line that would surely give her premature wrinkles. A shudder worked its way down her spine as she read the letter for the tenth time.

"God," she whispered, shaking her head.

This letter wasn't much different than the nineteen that had come before it. All had been annoying and slightly disturbing, but nothing major, because after all, she'd made more enemies than friends over the last couple of years. But this one terrified her. Made her feel overexposed and paranoid, as if someone were stalking her.

"Obviously someone is, dumbass," she muttered, willing her hand to stop trembling.

The envelope the letter had come in was white and this time, unlike all the other times, it was postmarked from Arlington, Virginia. Before, they'd come from the San Fernando Valley, California.

The letter itself was plain, cheap printer stock. Thin and without any embellishments. Didn't she deserve at least card stock and some elegant flowery border? She snorted, but the humor was short-lived. The words on the paper weren't funny.

Bitches like you don't deserve to live when all you do is ruin lives.

What a charming opening line, she thought. The letter went on from there, like the others, rambling about how she shouldn't be able to sleep at night and that he—she assumed it was a *he*—would be watching. The big difference this time, besides the fact that he'd found her in D.C., was the ending.

I'll be seeing you tonight.

Her breath caught and pressure seized her chest.

It didn't matter how many times she'd read that last line. Each time her eyes crawled across those five words, she felt the burn in her throat, the building in the back of her mouth. She wanted to scream, and she never screamed.

Placing the letter beside the others in a neat line, she then stood on weak legs. Her fingers icy and numb, she walked across the living room to the window overlooking the teeming street below. Traffic was snarled due to the rush hour and sidewalks were packed. Branches on a few late-blooming cherry blossoms in the distance swayed.

Her gaze moved from the faint pink blossoms to the people scurrying along the sidewalk and darting across the street, dodging taxis and towncars.

Could he be down there right this second, watching her? *No.*

She stopped herself from backing away from the window, from caving into fear, and squeezed her eyes shut. No way could she allow herself to think that. She'd end up like her mother then. She wouldn't let this . . . this *fucker* do this to her. Only *she* had control of her life and her choices.

"Focus," she said, rubbing tiny circles along her temples.

She twisted away from the window and opened her eyes. The room was minimalistic in design, muted colors of black and gray. As a kid, she'd wanted everything to be in Rainbow Brite colors. That was before she'd developed something called taste.

Or before she'd ended up with the stick up her ass.

Wasn't that what Chad had said to her once during her

4

assignment? He wouldn't have been the first to say it. Or the last.

Her heels clicked off the hardwood floor as she went back to the coffee table. She dropped her hands to her hips, her eyes narrowing behind her glasses. She had to fix this, gain control of the situation. It was the only option. But doing so required that she take the threats seriously. Ignoring these letters, like she had been for the last year, was like ignoring an ache that wouldn't go away. No good shit comes from that.

She needed to figure out who was behind these letters, and that wasn't going to be easy. Granny always said that her brass balls—*lovely*—were never going to win her any friends or a husband.

Apparently, they had won her a stalker, though.

That had to count for something.

Alana had quite the list of people who had reason to be upset with her, too. But to send her threatening letters for a year? The latest even going as far as to warn that he'd be seeing her *tonight*? Sure, she ticked people off with her hard-nosed tactics, but those facts had to narrow down the pool of suspects. While she had excellent sleuthing skills, that's not what she needed tonight.

She needed protection.

And she knew who to go to.

Hopefully he would be wearing more than boxers this time around. Although, she wasn't going to complain about the eyeful she had gotten when she'd tracked down Chad to his brother's house nearly three months ago.

Through the course of her career working with sports stars and actors, she had seen a lot of good-looking men—men who would have sensible women all across the nation dropping their panties. But that man, the eldest Gamble brother, had officially been the hottest male she'd ever laid eyes on. She wasn't sure if it was the wild shoulder-length hair or those startling blue eyes. Or it could've been those incredibly wide shoulders that would make any woman feel petite, or that rock-hard chest and those abs . . .

"What am I doing?" She smacked her forehead with her palm, pushing those thoughts aside.

Going to him for help had nothing to do with envisioning him in those boxers or showing off those hard, naked abs, no matter how touchable those abs appeared to be. And the last thing she needed to be doing right now was mentally molesting the man. It was highly unlikely that he'd be happy to see her, but he sort of owed her his services. She had played a rather excellent matchmaker when it came to his brother and Ms. Rodgers.

She was still waiting on *that* wedding invitation.

Scooping up the letters, Alana placed them inside a file folder labeled ASSHOLE and shoved the folder into her leather satchel. She left her apartment, in search of a very different type of asshole.

Chandler Gamble's phone vibrated in the pocket of his jeans for the second time in the last hour. He needed to continue ignoring it. He should ignore it. What was going on in front of him should have his undivided attention. Any other time, it would.

On her knees between his widespread legs, Paula was in a position he doubted she was normally in when it came to her day job, being a district attorney and all. She ran her hands up and down his thighs, each pass bringing the tips of her red-painted fingernails to the center of his legs. Her movements were well practiced. She knew what he liked.

The red corset she wore was laced up tight, practically shoving her caramel-colored breasts up to her chin. Some men were into breasts, others more about the ass. Chandler was into the female body in general. All of it. But when he was with Paula, he turned into a breast man. Those things were the stuff that wet dreams were made of.

But tonight? The last couple of months? The head on his shoulders was doing more thinking than any other place on his body, which was kind of a damn shame.

Paula slipped a hand up the inside of his thigh. "I've missed you."

He laughed, sliding farther down in the oversize cushioned chair, spreading his legs farther. "No you didn't."

Her pretty lips pouted. "You haven't come to see me since February. Or anyone, from what I've heard."

A brow rose. He didn't like the idea of anyone keeping tabs on him.

"You haven't even been to the club," she said.

"So?"

"That's not like you." She placed her hands on the chair between his legs, drawing his eyes down to her impressive chest. For some reason, he imagined much smaller breasts plumped up over the lacy trim and little bows.

And there were about a million different things wrong with that.

Irritated, he scrubbed the palm of his hand along his jaw.

The faint stubble pricked his skin. What the hell was wrong with him? He'd been at Leather and Lace for almost an hour now and by this time he would've already been behind a woman, his hands on her hips, sliding in and out.

"Want to talk?" she asked, pushing back from the chair and clasping her hands demurely.

He laughed drily. "No, honey, but thanks."

One delicate, satiny shoulder rose. "You sure? You're moody and quiet by nature, babe, but disappearing for months? I was worried."

Chandler bit back another laugh. That wasn't likely. Paula was good, great even. And their sexual . . . *tastes* matched, but when he wasn't around, there was *always* someone else. Like him, she enjoyed sex. Lots, really, except lately, he'd been only getting it on with his hand.

"I don't want to talk," he said again.

Thick lashes lowered as she toyed with the knot between her breasts. "No talking? I can do that."

He watched her rise fluidly. Paula was a tall woman, and in her "come fuck me" heels, she nearly reached his six feet and four inches. She pivoted gracefully, and he got an eyeful of her ass. The scrap of lace between her cheeks revealed more than it hid as she swayed her way over to the chaise longue across from him.

It was a nice view—a beautiful view. Paula's skin was like smooth coffee, and he knew from personal experience that an hour with that woman could make you forget a year of life, but . . .

Any other time he'd be as hard as a brick wall and ready to go . . . and to go again, but the lust stirring in his veins wasn't anything to write home about. He definitely wasn't feeling what little Miss Paula was.

She cast a look over her shoulder as she bit down on her lip. Still nothing at all. She placed a shapely knee on the lounge and bent over, planting her hands near the top of the chair, and then brought her other leg up. Nice—very nice.

And yet there was really nothing happening in his jeans.

Bending down, she stuck her ass in the air. "I think I've been naughty, Chandler."

He cocked a brow. "You have?"

She blinked innocently. "I think I need to be *punished*."

Fine, barely there tendrils of lust stirred in his gut. Okay. It was official. His cock had taken a vacay into celibacy land. Fuck. Him.

Tipping his head back, he stifled a groan. What in the fuck was he even doing here? It was either this or hang out with his brothers, and who in the hell in their right mind wanted to do that shit? All Chase and Chad talked about were their women. Not that he begrudged them their happiness, but shit, it was like hanging out with two old women. Especially since Chad was knee-deep in wedding plans.

And if he had to hear about the difference between ivory and white one more time, he was going to shoot someone.

Hell, ask him a year ago if he thought the playboy of the three of them would be the one to marry first, and he would've laughed straight in your face. But Chase was in love. And so was their pro baseball player brother, Chad. Despite the shit they'd dealt with growing up.

The thing was, and contrary to everyone's assumption of him—including his brothers— Chandler didn't have any problems with the idea of settling down. While those who were unaware of the Gamble brothers' upbringing thought Chandler was the most affected by it due to his . . . *habits* and the fact he rarely stayed with one woman, truth was, he had enough common sense to know that not all relationships were like his parents'. Spending time with the Daniels family—Chase's fiancée's family—had helped prove that men and women could live happily together and all that shit. In reality, he had always been the least affected by his bastard of a father and train wreck of a mother.

He just hadn't met the woman he wanted to be with for more than a few hours here and there or involve in any aspect of his life.

Yes, you have, whispered an annoying-as-fuck voice.

Yeah, he was going to push that thought right out of his head.

He really should get the fuck out of here. The lack of interest was one of the reasons why he hadn't frequented Leather and Lace lately. And this was the only place he'd do this in. He never brought women back to his home. In fact, Chad's ex–publicist from hell had been the only woman to ever get a pretty little foot through his front door.

His cell started vibrating again.

Jesus H. Christ.

Leaning back in his chair, he reached into his pocket and pulled out his cell. Curiosity perked when he saw that it was his office number. "Murray?"

"Thanks for answering the phone in a timely manner," a deep, gravelly voice said.

Chandler's lips tipped up at the corners. "I've been busy."

Which was utter bullshit, since all he'd been doing was sitting here, staring at a half-naked woman, with the limpest dick in town. "What's up?"

"There was this *lady* here looking for you."

He arched a brow as Paula glanced over her bare shoulder again and licked her plump red lips. "Did she say what she needed?"

"I'd assume she was looking to hire us. Actually, you," he replied, and the sound of fingers tapping along a keyboard echoed in the background. "She asked for you directly."

Strange. Most people who came looking for his services didn't ask for him. He owned and ran CCG Security, and on very rare cases, he took the jobs instead of letting his team handle them. Very rare. "What's her name?"

"She didn't leave one."

"And you didn't ask?" His brows lowered.

Murray snorted. "Of course I did, but she didn't give it to me. And before you ask, she was out the door and down the street before I could get my gimpy ass out of the chair and follow her to get her tags."

About three weeks ago, Murray had taken a nasty gunshot to the leg during a security detail in Chicago and was now on desk duty for at least another three weeks. Shit happened. Chandler had a matching bullet wound on his arm and his thigh from an incident a few years back.

Shaking her lace-covered ass at him, Paula purred softly.

All right. That managed to get his attention. His jeans tightened by the slightest measure, but still. He got this hard when he saw a 1969 Dodge Charger in mint condition.

Shit.

Maybe he needed to see his doctor about low testosterone or something.

"What did she look like?" he asked, sliding forward on the chair as he sent Paula an apologetic look.

Murray sighed. "Mean."

"Mean?"

"Mean as in cup your balls, she's a scary lady."

A strange feeling crawled up the back of his neck. "What did she look like, Murray? A bit more descriptive, if you have the time."

"She had dark hair—dark brown with matching dark eyes. Wore glasses," he went on, and Chandler's hand tightened around the slim phone. "Wearing a black pantsuit and black heels. I could tell you that she looked plain, but also like the kind of woman—"

"Did she leave a number or anything?" he interrupted, that strange sensation now crawling over his skull. Muscles clenched in his stomach.

"Nope. She bounced like a ball when I said you weren't here."

His mouth opened, but there were no words. The image that came to mind was Miss Gore. Sounded like her, but that made no sense. There was no reason why she would seek him out. Not like she didn't know where his brother Chad, her former client, lived.

It couldn't be her.

"Call me immediately if she comes back," he said.

Murray laughed. "That's what I've been doing. Try answering the phone next time."

There wasn't much Chandler could say to that. He hung

up, sliding the phone back into his pocket. His mind was still on the conversation, on the bizarre possibility . . .

"Are you okay?" Paula asked, startling him.

He blinked and nodded.

"Then come join me. I'm getting lonely over here."

Without thinking about it, he stood and slowly made his way over to the chaise longue. When he looked down at Paula, it wasn't her he saw. The picture that formed in his mind? Well, he'd like to say it came out of nowhere, but it hadn't. He'd seen it a time or two since that annoying publicist showed up at his door, looking for Chad.

Kneeling on the longue was Miss Gore. Dressed in that damn black pantsuit. Except her hair was down, falling around her face in dark waves. The glasses were on. He liked the glasses.

And now Chandler was hard as that fucking brick wall he'd been thinking about earlier.

Good news? His dick worked.

Bad news? Shit. There was a lot of bad in this.

Paula's gaze dipped below his belt, and her eyes lit up. "That for me?"

Uh. No.

He opened his mouth, but the door swung open unexpectedly and his chin jerked up, eyes narrowing. No one in this club would barge into any of these rooms unless they were invited. There were rules, for chrissakes, and . . .

Holy shit.

In the dim red glow of the small overhead light, a slight form appeared like an apparition, straight out of the shadows and out of his fantasies.

Miss Gore stood just inside the room, clenching a folder to her chest like some kind of shield. Behind her glasses, her eyes moved from him to Paula and back again. A pink blush bled into her cheeks, and screw him, he got *harder*.

Her expression remained cool, though, as she cleared her throat. "We need to talk."

Chapter Two

Anyone who had ever met Alana Gore and was around her for ten minutes would agree that she was determined and impatient. Those two things made for a nasty combination.

And could lead to really awkward situations.

When she'd gone to the offices of CCG Security and was told that Chandler wasn't there, her next stop had been his house. Of course, there'd been no answer there, either, and while Leather and Lace had been a shot in the dark, it had been one she'd been willing to take. While she'd poked around in Chad Gamble's personal activities several months ago, she'd discovered this "exclusive club" in the Foggy Bottom district. The middle brother was known to frequent the club every once in a while, but Chandler was a regular, from what she'd discovered.

Leather and Lace was nothing more than a sex club fronting as a regular nightclub, and as much as Alana wanted to be disgusted by the whole thing, she couldn't help the slight wiggle of curiosity whenever she thought about the place and what went on inside the rooms on the second floor. Were there really people hooking up and engaging in all kinds of sexual play inside?

Well, now she knew for sure.

Her gaze crawled between Chandler and the barely dressed woman on her hands and knees. Alana doubted she was searching for a missing contact lens dressed in a corset and little else. Unless her clothing had fallen off in the process.

Alana's stare lingered on the woman's chest, and she suddenly felt like she was rocking a training bra. Christ on a crutch, were those things real? Her gaze finally drifted up to the woman's face and something about the pretty features was familiar . . . Holy fuck balls, wasn't she a district attorney?

Oh my.

Chandler cleared his throat, drawing her attention back to him. "We need to talk? Right now?"

For a moment, she couldn't speak. Her brief encounters with the elder Gamble brother hadn't served her memory well. Good God, this man . . .

His dark brown hair was loose, brushing broad shoulders that seemed bigger now that she was seeing him in person. His cheekbones were well defined and high, setting off a strong jawline and wide, expressive lips. While the other two Gamble brothers were lean, Chandler was taller and built like a heavyweight boxer.

Her gaze traveled down his throat, over the gap in his shirt at his neck, and then down his arms. The sleeves of his shirt were rolled up, exposing powerful forearms and large hands.

"Miss Gore?" Amusement colored Chandler's voice.

Heat flooded her cheeks. Dear God, was she *flustered*?

16

She was never flustered. An obnoxious giggle was building in her throat. Shit. Giggling? That ticked her off. Latching onto the irritation, she regained the use of her brain. "I know I'm interrupting ... important business, but this can't wait."

"Is that so?" Chandler shifted his weight, and it was only then that she realized he was standing behind the woman. Was he about to ... ?

Oh Lord in heaven, she couldn't finish that thought. "Yes. I need to talk to you in private."

Chandler said nothing.

She looked at the woman who had at least sat up, demurely crossing her legs, and then back at Chandler. Did she have to point out they weren't alone? By the expectant look on his face, she was going to go with a yes. "We're not alone."

"And you weren't in here first." A small grin appeared on those lips. Just one side tipping up. "It would be rude of me to ask my friend to leave, and I wouldn't want to be rude."

Alana's spine stiffened. Something about his tone told her that he was messing with her for his amusement. "I seriously doubt she's your friend."

"And what do you think she is to me, Miss Gore?" When she opened her mouth, his blue eyes sharpened. "And think carefully before you make a statement."

She bristled. "I'm not crude, Mr. Gamble."

"Really? That's not what I've heard."

A different kind of heat invaded her veins, and her fingers bit into the folder. The soft crinkle of paper reminded her why she was here, which was not to get into a verbal pissing match with Chandler. Taking a deep breath, she leveled her voice. "I need your help."

Chandler's chin tipped down, but his expression remained the same: remote and impassive. Not an ounce of emotion. Something about him, the intensity that he bled into the air around him, told her that this man would be a violent storm if he ever lost control.

Silence stretched out between them, broken by the soft, impatient sigh of the dark-skinned woman sitting on the chaise longue. It struck Alana then, in a way it hadn't before, what she was doing. Coming to Chandler for help had seemed logical while she'd been in her apartment, as she knew he would be discreet in his services, but busting up in a sex club looking for him?

Ah, probably not the wisest of decisions. Not to mention supremely awkward, but there wasn't anything she could do about that now. The letter had rattled her. *I'll be seeing you tonight.* Finding Chandler couldn't wait, but now?

Holding her head high, she stepped back. "Perhaps another time will be better. When you're not about to engage in hopefully protected sex." She smiled tightly. "Good evening, Mr. Gamble and ... uh, Miss ... That's a really nice corset."

The woman smiled. "Thank you."

Alana made it to the door, feeling an odd burn in her skin. Humiliation? It had been a long, long time since she'd felt that way, and she didn't much care for it now, either.

"Miss Gore." Chandler's deep voice stopped her.

She turned halfway. "What?"

He glanced at the woman. "I'm sorry, honey, but maybe we can pick this up again later?"

"I understand." The woman stood, and at once, Alana felt like she belonged in the Lollipop Guild. The woman strode past her, smiling. "*Work* is work."

Was that a dig? Alana couldn't be sure, but then the door shut quietly behind her, and she was alone in the room with the guy she admittedly had fantasized about a time or two or twenty. In a room that he had most likely been about to have wild, lustful, animal-like, noise-making sex in. At that thought, an image of her on that chaise longue with Chandler behind her, his hands gripping her hips, filled her head. Warmth sparked in her belly and much, much lower.

She really needed to get control of herself.

Clearing her throat, she met his stare and flushed at the almost knowing gleam in his blue eyes. "You didn't have to make her leave. We could've—"

"I think it was obvious that she needed to leave," he cut in, crossing his arms across his broad chest. "So what is it that you need help with, Miss Gore?"

"But I was interrupting."

He arched an eyebrow. "And I'm sure you knew that before you burst through that door, right?"

"Well, yes, but—" Actually, no. She hadn't thought of anything except getting to Chandler. She refused to examine why the thought of reaching him had been the only thing that had calmed her pulse since receiving the letter.

"But you now have my full, undivided attention." Chandler took one step forward, and sweet Jesus, he was right in front of her. It had to be those long legs that seemed to eat up the distance in one stride. "And that is a very, very rare occurrence."

Swallowing again, she felt her gaze nervously flit over his shoulder. What the . . . ? Were those *handcuffs* hanging against the wall? She was totally out of her element and off her game. Who could blame her? She was in a room used for all kinds of kinky sexual acts.

"I need your help," she said, relieved to hear her voice was somewhat steady.

He unfolded his arms, and as he did, the rolled-up sleeves of his shirt brushed her hands, causing her body to jerk. That one-sided smile spread. "I think we've already established that, Miss Gore."

Irritation pricked at her skin, mostly at herself for becoming so frazzled. "I have a problem." When his brows shot up, she wanted to smack her face with the file folder. Had she lost brain cells somewhere between entering this room and right now? Fuck. "I've been receiving threatening letters."

Chandler didn't respond, so she shoved the file folder toward him, which wasn't very far, since he was in her personal space and then some. He didn't take it, and her irritation grew into frustration. "They're all in here—twenty of them."

"Okay." He drew out the word as his gaze dipped. But not to her hands. To her chest.

Alana didn't know what to think or say at that point. She was a logical woman. A minute ago, he had had a woman in here who had two baby butts for boobs and she was barely a B cup. Not to mention there was no way in holy hell he could see her goods. She was wearing a white blouse buttoned straight up to her chin and a suit jacket. Unless he had x-ray vision, he was just being an ass.

Struggling to get a grip on her quickly rising anger, she snapped the file folder against his chest. "Do you want to look at them? Or do you want to continue staring at my breasts like a pig?"

That ghost of a smile spread into a full smirk. "I think I'll keep staring at your breasts like a pig."

"Well, that's lovely."

"They sure are," he replied.

Alana took one deep, even breath. "Mr. Gamble, I'm here—"

"Because you need my help," he interrupted. "I got that."

"And I'm trying to show you what I've been receiving." She smacked the folder off his chest once again. "So can we—"

His hand shot out, as fast as a cobra striking, startling her. He wrapped his fingers around her wrist, gently but firmly. Lowering his head, he brought his lips to within an inch of hers. So close she could taste the minty scent of his breath. "While I like to be smacked in the chest with random objects from time to time, you keep it up, I'm going to think that's an invitation for me to return the favor."

Her mouth dropped open.

"On a different part of the body," he added, winking. "And with my hand."

She gasped and her skin burned, but not from embarrassment. Oh no. The mere thought of his hand on her ass almost had her forgetting why she came here. Almost. She jerked her arm free, knowing he simply allowed her to do so. "That was extremely unprofessional."

Chandler laughed deeply, sending a shiver down her spine, and spread his arms wide. "What about any of this would be considered professional?"

He had a good point, but still. She took a step back, which grated on her nerves. "Mr. Gamble, I am trying to—"

"Say it."

Having no idea where he was going with that statement, she shook her head. "Say what?"

"My name."

Her brows knitted as she stared up at him. "I do believe I've been saying your name. Perhaps all that muscle and hair are impairing your hearing."

He chuckled again as he stalked forward, reclaiming the distance between them. "That wasn't very nice, *Alana*."

At the sound of her name rolling off his tongue, the muscles in her stomach tightened. "What? Do you want me to say your first name?"

"Yes, actually, I do."

She rolled her eyes. "Well, no thank you. I prefer to keep this businesslike."

"Again, what about this is business appropriate?" He moved his arms out to his sides once more, gesturing around him. "The handcuffs? Or the lovers' swing folded in the corner? Or the lounge, which comes complete with stirrups?"

Oh dear Lord . . .

"Or the fact you hunted me down?"

Her lips mashed together. "I didn't *hunt* you down. It wasn't that hard to find you. After all, if you weren't at your office, home, or with your brothers, where else would you be but at a club with such a stellar reputation?"

He cocked his head to the side. "Have you been stalking me, Alana?"

"It is Miss Gore to you, and no, I'm not stalking you." She took another deep breath. "Are you going to listen to me or continue to derail the conversation?"

"I wasn't aware that's what I was doing," he said. "I've been following along easily. You've been receiving threatening letters, which I assume are in the folder you keep using as a weapon, but I'm not sure how I can be of any help with that."

She stared at him a moment, absolutely baffled. "Doesn't it seem obvious? You run a company that specializes in personal security. I'm coming here because obviously I need security."

Another deep laugh erupted from him, but this time, it didn't make her warm on the inside. "I'm not sure if you understand the kind of security we offer."

Bristling, she tipped up her chin. "I'm sure I do."

He shook his head slowly. "We offer security to people who are under a real threat, Alana. Those who have received death threats or have had attempts on their lives made— attempts made by very serious and very deadly people."

"How do you know attempts haven't been made or that I haven't received death threats?" she demanded, clinging to her temper with a fine thread. "You've been too busy ogling me and making sexual innuendoes."

23

"Back to your breasts?"

The base of her neck was starting to tingle. "Oh my God."

"You brought them up. Both times. Not me." A quick grin flashed across his face. "And if attempts were made on your life, you wouldn't be here showing me letters. And while I'm sure you have a list as long as my arm consisting of people you've pissed off, I doubt any of them are a serious threat."

Her eyes narrowed. "How would you know that?"

"Oh, I don't know. Maybe it's because you blackmailed my brother's fiancée and nearly drove him insane?"

A bit of heat peaked on her cheeks. "Whatever. Look at them now. They're getting married. They should be thanking me."

He shot her a dry look. "How many other people have you *helped* like that?"

She wanted to feign innocence at the question, but she knew better. So did Chandler. His accusations made her uncomfortable in ways he probably couldn't even fathom. "Look, I need to hire someone who can be discreet and—"

"I can't," he interrupted.

"What?" Surprise shuttled through her. "Why not?"

Chandler's lashes lowered, shielding his eyes. "Several reasons, but mainly, there's a rule that all my employees operate by, as do I."

"Which is?"

"Under no circumstances do any of my employees or I take a job that has a conflict of interest."

Confused, she held the folder closer to her chest. "Is your brother a conflict of interest?"

He shook his head, and a moment passed before he answered. "No. We don't protect anyone we want to fuck."

Chapter Three

The moment those words came out of his mouth, Chandler knew he meant them. Maybe when they'd first formed on his tongue, he was saying them just to mess with her, but there was something about Miss Gore that brought out a teasing side of him. She'd gotten under his skin from the first moment he'd met her.

Alana opened and closed her mouth a couple of times, drawing his attention to that interesting part of her face. Her lips were devoid of any makeup, not even a faint trace of faded lipstick, but they were fuller than he remembered, and he bet they'd be soft if they weren't always in such a tense, tight line.

"I'm going to pretend you didn't say that," she said, her voice unsurprisingly level.

He wondered if anything truly got to the woman. "I'm not going to pretend."

"This . . . That was . . . That is so inappropriate that I don't even know where to begin." She reached up, taking off her glasses. For the briefest second, he saw her face for the first time without them before she placed them back on.

Her eyes were dark, nearly black, but they were less cold

without the glass barrier between them and the world. The skin around her eyes was free from wrinkles, and her lashes were thick, incredibly long. He leaned back, his gaze searching her face. She scrunched her nose and still, her skin barely crinkled. With the slight pink flush staining her cheeks, she looked youthful—younger than he ever imagined. His eyes narrowed.

"How old are you?" he asked, suddenly realizing that she couldn't be as old as he originally believed.

"What?" She pinched the bridge of her nose, squeezing her eyes shut.

He cocked his head to the side, brows lowering. "How old are you?"

"How old are *you*?" she shot back.

"I'm thirty-three. Answer my damn question."

"You're giving me a headache." She slid her glasses back on. "My age has nothing to do with why I'm here." She paused and then added under her breath, "I don't even know why I'm here."

Annoyed, because he was used to people doing what he wanted, he folded his arms. "Why won't you just answer the question?"

"Why would I? You don't want to work for me. Do you need to make sure I'm of legal age for a good fucking? Because I can tell you two things you can take to the bank." Her free hand formed a little fist. "I'm definitely of legal age, and your dick isn't coming within spitting distance of any part of my body."

A smile tugged at his lips. "What an incredible mouth you have on you."

She stared at him for a good half a minute and then exploded like a bottle rocket. "For fuck's sake, talking to you is impossible! Fucking forget I even came here, because this was the most pointless trip I've ever made in the history of fucking forever!"

He blinked, surprised by her outburst. And turned on—completely, 100 percent rocking a raging hard-on. There was definitely something wrong with that, but he wasn't surprised. He liked his women mouthy.

And this one was a volcano.

The volcano was also leaving.

Alana yanked at the door and nearly threw herself off balance. Paula must've locked it on her way out, something they should've thought about earlier, but then again, Chandler couldn't find it in himself to regret Alana's interruption.

Cursing up a storm under her breath, she unlocked the door and tore it open. Within seconds, she'd disappeared into the shadowy hall outside the private room.

Chandler started after her but stopped.

"Shit," he muttered, thrusting his fingers through his hair.

He needed to let her go. What he knew about her, which wasn't much but definitely enough, was that the woman would be nothing but trouble. That was the last thing he needed in his life right now. It didn't matter that her appearance had his cock waking from its majorly inconvenient slumber. And the most messed-up thing was that he was still hard.

Damn, she had smelled good. The scent of a flower that reminded him of spring, but he couldn't place what it was.

And now he was thinking about how she smelled. Fuuuucck.

Letting her go back to wherever she came from was the smartest thing he could do. For that matter, what the hell was she still doing in this city? Her assignment as his brother's publicist had ended in January and from what he'd gathered from Chad, she lived in California. So why was she still here?

Did it even matter?

Chandler told himself that it didn't, but—and there always seemed to be a but—what if she was in trouble? And he'd just told her he'd rather fuck her than protect her? He didn't feel bad about saying that, but Jesus, he hadn't even looked at those letters.

He bit out a ripe curse. Letters were not serious. The kind of shit he saw and dealt with on a regular basis made threatening letters something a child would do. Not to mention the fact that Alana had to have a list as long as his leg when it came to enemies who wanted to scare her.

Of course, none of this made him any less of a jackass right now.

Dropping his hand, he shook his head. Receiving threatening letters didn't warrant a personal security detail in any situation. He hadn't been kidding around when he'd told her they protected people being threatened by very dangerous individuals, but a twinge of guilt still churned in his stomach. He hadn't taken her seriously, hadn't even listened to her story.

"Shit," he said again.

* * *

29

The back of Alana's throat burned as she made her way across the crowded club floor. Even if she wasn't speed walking, she'd stand out among the patrons of Leather and Lace. Her prim black suit was an eyesore among the shimmery tops, skintight jeans, and pretty dresses.

So plain. So boring.

Normally, that wouldn't bother her, but tonight, she felt like all her emotions were on the outside, coating her skin instead of being neatly tucked away.

A hand grabbed for her as she rounded a cluster of small tables. She shot a warning look at the offender, a young male with kohl-lined eyes. He simply laughed and threw an arm over the shoulders of a petite redhead.

To Alana, the air in the club was suffocating—hot and heavy with the scent of perfume, cologne, and liquor. She barreled out the front door, gasping in the cool night air as it washed over her flushed skin.

Stupid—she had been so incredibly stupid coming here, thinking that Chandler would actually agree to help her. His crude statement of wanting to have sex with her was most likely nothing more than an attempt to get a rise out of her.

He'd succeeded.

Even though things had worked out splendidly for Chad and Bridget, she *had* blackmailed them. It was doubtful that any of Chad's brothers or friends would feel warm and fuzzy when it came to her.

But she'd just been doing her job. That's what she kept telling herself as she hurried down the sidewalk, passing the graffiti-sprayed exteriors of the old warehouses.

What was she going to do now?

I'll be seeing you tonight.

Her practical mind clicked over, taking control. She was on her own, something she'd grown accustomed to in her twenty-six years. You could really only count on yourself—trite but true. So she'd need to find out who was responsible for stalking her clear across the country, and she also needed a gun. Then she needed to know how to use one, because she honestly had no idea how to even take off the safety and—

Rounding the street corner, she winced as she realized that two of the overhead streetlamps were now out and the packed parking lot was nothing more than hulking, looming shadows and a cesspool of potential assault and battery.

Great. Getting stabbed and robbed would be the icing on the fucked-up cake and make her night.

Digging the car keys out of her pocket, she threaded them between her fingers and kept her eyes peeled for any suspicious movement. She picked up her pace, focusing on the third line of cars where she'd left hers.

The parking lot nearest to Leather and Lace was like a used luxury-car lot. She passed Audis, Volvos, BMWs, and a whole fleet of foreign vehicles. Alana was willing to bet her relatively flat ass that half the city's power players were members of the club.

She wanted to be all kinds of judging, but she was the type of person to call a spade a spade. How could she judge them when she had been inside that room with Chandler, picturing herself on the longue?

Unwanted heat unfurled low in her belly, and she swore softly as she cut between a Mercedes and an Infiniti SUV.

She would not think about Chandler. She would not give that son of a bitch one more ounce of her—

Alana stopped a few feet before her Lexus, her breath expelling harshly. It was so dark here she couldn't be sure what she was seeing. Bending at the waist, she blinked once, thinking that her eyes were playing tricks on her, but when her vision centered on the front of her car, she cried out in disbelief.

The windshield had been smashed in.

Jagged edges of glass remained, but the whole center was gone—completely gone. Wicked sharp pieces of glass lay on the dashboard.

Her breaths came out in short pants as she reached down and opened the driver's door. Glass was everywhere—on the seats, the floorboards. She started to reach in but stopped herself. Lying on the passenger seat was a brick. There appeared to be a paper wrapped around it, secured with a rubber band.

For a moment, Alana was absolutely frozen. She didn't move. Her breath stilled in her throat. All she could do was stare at that brick, and the only thing that moved was her heart. It thumped heavily in her chest, sending adrenaline coursing through her veins.

Her gaze crawled over the interior and then widened when she saw the ignition. The whole lower part of the steering wheel had been torn open, wires exposed and dangling like little red and blue snakes.

"Oh my God," she whispered, slowly shaking her head. She couldn't believe what she was seeing.

Anger poured into her chest, causing her hand to tighten

around the keys until the metal dug into flesh. Someone had done this to *her* car—*her* property. No way in hell did she believe this was coincidental. It had to be the asshole behind the letters, and . . .

Icy fear snapped at the heels of her fury. Her breath came out in a ragged exhale. The person who had done this could still be here, waiting and watching. *Oh my God.* Her heart jumped in her chest painfully. Backing away from her car door, she scanned the darkness ahead of her.

She swallowed, but the knot of fear made it difficult. She was out here, alone, and if someone wanted—

A heavy hand landed on her shoulder.

Shrieking, she spun around, dropping the folder and throwing out her hand that held the key-shank she'd created.

"Jesus H. Christ, woman!" a deep voice exploded as a hand clamped down on her wrist.

Part of her brain recognized the voice, but the adrenaline and fear had kicked in her fight response and once that had been unleashed, it was taking her brain precious seconds to catch up to how her body was reacting.

She tried to pull her arm free as she raised her knee, aiming for any body part she could do damage on. Hopefully the gonads.

Except she never connected with any flesh.

A second later, her back was against the SUV parked beside her car and a broad, firm body was pressed against hers. Thick, muscled legs made it impossible for her to kick. Both her wrists were captured in a secure hold, pinned near her shoulders in record time. The keys hit the ground somewhere down by her feet.

Good God, she had been incapacitated that quickly.

It would've been rather impressive if she wasn't seconds away from having a full-blown heart attack.

"Are you done?" he asked, his voice carrying a hard edge. "You could've taken my eye out."

As her heart rate slowed down, her brain finally started to work again. Lifting her head, she found herself face-to-face with Chandler once more. Not just face-to-face, but mostly body-to-body.

"Sorry," she croaked out hoarsely and then wondered why in the hell she was apologizing. "You scared me! You snuck up on me."

"Snuck up on you?" A muscle ticked in his jaw, visible even in the poor lighting. "I wasn't sneaking. I'm not part ninja."

Considering she hadn't heard him, she begged to differ on that statement. And the man had the reflexes of a jungle cat. "Part ninja or not, it's nighttime and you put your hand on me in the middle of a dark parking lot without warning. Excuse me for—"

"Overreacting?" he suggested, dark brows lowered. "Is this how you normally respond?"

Were they actually going to argue about this? From the look of it, the answer would be yes. Her fingers curled helplessly and she drew in a deep breath. The action brought her breasts flush with his chest, and she couldn't stop the electrical jolt that zinged through her, nor the way her nipples hardened at the sensation.

Oh goodness, her reaction was wholly wrong, all things considered.

34

She was going to blame residual trauma from seeing her car obliterated. "Let go of me," she said, taking another breath and immediately wishing she hadn't. The jolt hit her again, stronger. "Now."

"I don't know about that." And just like that, Chandler's demeanor shifted. Everything about him changed. His body relaxed in a way that said he was ready to snap into action but was solely focused on her. The lines of his face softened, and his eyes took on a hooded, lazy quality. "You might try to shank me again."

A whole different set of warnings went off in the back of her head as the air became rife with the kind of tension that had nothing to do with the car or the fact that she'd almost blinded him in the eye moments before. Nearly every part of their bodies that mattered was lined up. His breath was warm against her forehead, and around her wrists, his thumbs began to move in slow, idle circles. A fine shiver skated over her skin as her pulse fluttered under his fingers. Everything he did, from the way he held her against the car to how his intense stare reached in, captured, and then seared her, oozed raw, almost primitive sexuality. Never had she come across anyone who affected her on such a level. It had been that way the first time she'd met him and then again at his brother's apartment.

Chandler shifted his hips, and she sucked in a sharp breath. She felt him against her belly, long and hard. Heat simmered low in her stomach and then dropped lower, like it had inside the room. Except they hadn't been touching then, and while he really wasn't doing anything now, her body was reacting to his in a way that shocked her.

This was so not the appropriate time for this. Even though she doubted anyone would come after her now that Chandler was here—and if anyone did, he most definitely had a death wish—but still. There were more important things to be focusing on.

But instinct was telling her that if she tipped her head back farther, Chandler would gladly accept the unspoken invitation. It wouldn't matter that they barely knew each other. He'd already stated quite clearly what he wanted from her, much to her disbelief. He would kiss her, and she already knew that she'd be kissed in a way she'd never experienced before.

Her heart tripped up over the thought of his lips moving against hers. One kiss and she'd be putty in his no-doubt-skilled hands. Alana wasn't easy, but with this man, she'd probably throw herself onto her own back.

His hands dropped from her wrists, landing on her hips, and as he leaned in, his nose grazed her cheek, snapping her out of her stupor. What in God's name was she doing?

Placing her hands against his chest—an incredibly hard chest—she pushed. "Back off, buddy."

He stepped away and opened his mouth, but then seemed to rethink what he was about to say. He finally checked out her car, frowning when he saw her open door. As he moved forward, she gulped in air and ignored the smidgen of disappointment.

"What in the hell?" he said, facing her car fully. Gripping the door, he bent at the waist. "Looks like you lost a windshield."

She rolled her eyes. "No shit."

He cast a look over his shoulders that would've sent men running in the opposite direction. Alana made a face. "The sarcasm isn't necessary," he said before turning back to her car. "Man, they did a number on this baby. Looks like someone was trying to get himself a free ride."

She snorted. "You must be the muscle of your company and not the brains."

Again, he shot her another dark look, which she ignored.

"Ten minutes ago I told you that I was receiving threatening letters. Do you really think those two things aren't connected? Wait. Don't bother answering, because you could give two shits about that."

He stared at her, his eyes nearly black in the darkness. "Miss Gore . . ." His voice was a low warning.

"Because the only thing you were concerned with back in that—that *club*, was getting laid."

He made a noise in the back of his throat that sounded like a growl. "That wasn't the only thing I was concerned about."

"Whatever." She coughed out what probably sounded like a half-crazed laugh.

Kneeling down, she swooped up her keys and started picking up the letters that had slipped out of the file. "Why are you out here anyway? Did you want to check out my ass this time around?"

He sighed. "Actually, I was following you."

Her brows rose as she stood. Then she saw that he was holding the brick in his large hands. She forced her gaze to his face. "Why were you following me?"

"To check out your ass."

Alana entertained a brief fantasy of kicking him between the legs. "Okay. You know what, I obviously have a few phone calls to make, and I'm probably going to need that brick, since it's evidence and— Hey! What are you doing?"

"You can call the cops, but all they're going to do is file a vandalism report. Nothing more. And that's not going to do very much for you." Ignoring her as she reached for the brick again, he pulled off the rubber band, snapping the elastic, and a piece flung somewhere into the great beyond. Tossing the brick aside, he unfolded the piece of paper. Under the flickering street lamp, she could see the stationary, and knots of unease blossomed in her stomach.

No way—absolutely no way.

"Bitch," Chandler said, glancing up. His lips formed a thin, tight line. "Lovely."

Alana took a step back and then slumped against the SUV. "Shit."

He was suddenly beside her, his hand on her shoulder. "Alana?"

She couldn't tear her eyes away from the piece of paper he held in his other hand. There had been a tiny part of her that had hoped it was a random coincidence, but now she knew it wasn't. She hadn't noticed when it had been wrapped around the brick, but in the faint light and unfolded, she recognized the one-sided design—the black and white lines that crawled up the sides of the ivory sheet and the tiny flowers in each corner.

Fingers appeared under her chin, guiding her head up with surprising gentleness. "Are you okay?"

Not really. Her heart was beating way too fast again.

Dizziness swept through her as her eyes locked with Chandler's. A fine sheen of sweat dotted her forehead. There was a good chance she was going to be sick.

"Alana?" Real concern colored his tone as he slid his hand to the side of her neck, as if he was about to check her pulse. "Come on, baby, say something."

"The paper the note is written on—that paper is *mine*," she said. "It's from my home."

"Back in California?" he asked, his thumb doing its magic again, but this time on her neck.

"No—my apartment. Here in the city."

39

Chapter Four

Chandler was officially worried.

Alana hadn't spoken a word since he'd gotten the directions to her apartment out of her. Considering how mouthy and absolutely frustrating she usually was, silence from her had to be a bad thing.

He glanced at her as he came to a stoplight, the red from the light glaring across her profile. She was staring out the window, worrying her bottom lip. Her arms were folded, keeping the file tight against her chest like a shield.

She hadn't protested when he called Murray to get a tow truck out here. And she also hadn't questioned why he hadn't contacted the police.

He knew they'd probably treat her the same way he had when she'd asked for his help. Well, with the exception of the "wanting to fuck" comment. Sure, they'd go to her place and check it over—at some point tonight. The city was teeming with crime, and vandalism and a possible break-in wouldn't be high on their list of concerns.

God, he felt like a giant ass for outright dismissing her.

He wasn't convinced that her life was in danger—letters and a vandalized car didn't equal deadly intent—but something was definitely going on. What exactly and how far this was going to go, he wasn't sure yet. The note was folded in his pocket, practically burning a hole in it. He wanted to look at it again, see if there was anything else except the one word. His initial assumption could still be spot-on. Nothing too serious—maybe a pissed-off ex-boyfriend or client, and not something to hire a bodyguard over. But if her apartment really had been broken into, then that was a different story.

There was a part of Chandler, he recognized, that just wanted this all to be a bunch of nothing. The thought of someone seriously wanting to hurt the woman sitting quietly next to him twisted his gut in ways he didn't want to consider. It was much better for his peace of mind to figure this was the prank of some disgruntled ex-client than something far more dangerous.

Chandler pulled his truck into the parking garage attached to the high-rise apartments. His immediate observation of the building noted several security hazards. It was a good district, not known for a lot of serious crime, but there was no doorman that he saw, which meant anyone could come and go as they pleased. There didn't appear to be any security cameras at the garage entrance or inside, at least none that was obvious and would deter potential perpetrators. The lighting sucked in the garage, making it easy for anyone to be hiding. He didn't like any of it.

As he parked the truck and killed the engine, he looked over at her. "You doing okay?" The question made him strangely uncomfortable.

She finally met his gaze and nodded curtly. "I'm fine."

That was debatable.

Clearing her throat, she reached for the door handle. "Thank you for taking me home, but I can call the police and let them handle it from here on out."

"I came all this way, so I'm going to check out your apartment."

She was out of his truck with surprising quickness, slamming the door.

He cursed under his breath and climbed out, finding her standing near his side, hand extended.

"I'm going to need the note, please." Her voice was clipped, professional, and cool.

His eyes narrowed. Instead of handing it over, he walked around her and headed toward the elevator entrance. "I'm checking out your apartment and then we're going to talk. And I'm serious. I'm not arguing with you."

There was a moment when he thought she was going to stand there and he was going to have to go back and drag her to her apartment.

"Damn it, you're annoying." She huffed, catching up to him. "Pain in my ass."

His lips twitched as he fought the smile. "I would love to be in your—"

"Don't even finish that statement," she snapped.

He chuckled, happy to see a little color returning to her cheeks. "What floor?"

"Sixteen." She was quiet as they stepped into the elevator. "Are you taking me seriously now?"

Chandler didn't immediately respond, and she made a sound that reminded him of a disgruntled animal—a small, helpless animal. When they reached her floor, she told him her number. "Stay by the elevator until I give you the okay," he said.

Her eyes narrowed. "Why?"

"Because I say so." He started toward her door but stopped. "I mean it, Alana. Stay here."

She inhaled deeply. "Fine. Staying."

He held her stare for a moment and then headed toward her door. Trying the handle, he found that it was locked. That was a good sign. "Throw me your keys."

Reaching into her pocket, she pulled out the keys, smiled, and then threw them.

Right at his face.

He caught them a second before impact. She smirked when his eyes narrowed. He had a feeling that if he were in her presence for another fifteen minutes, she was going to end up over his knee.

Grappling for patience he typically didn't afford people, he unlocked her door and then slipped the keys into his pocket. He needed his hand free for something else. Reaching around to his back, he withdrew his Glock.

"You have a gun?" she hissed, eyes wide.

He shot her a droll look. "My job sort of requires that, and I said, stay by the elevator."

She opened her mouth, but then clicked it shut as she backed away, holding that damn file to her chest. He sent her one last look of warning and then edged into her apartment. It was doubtful that anyone was still here, but he wanted to make sure before she stepped one annoying foot into the apartment.

Moving silently down the short entryway, he checked out the kitchen. A sliding glass door led out to a balcony, which was attached to a fire escape. Not good. The door was latched from the inside, but he knew from experience that anyone could strong-arm one of these mothers right open. He then shifted his attention to the living room.

A small lamp was on next to a couch, casting a soft glow. He wasn't surprised by the simple, minimalistic design and how there didn't seem to be a pillow out of place on the couch or a single piece of anything on the floor. Ms. Stick-up-her-ass probably never had a shoe out of place.

Ruling the living room and kitchen empty, he proceeded down a hallway, checking out a bathroom and an office before entering the master bedroom. The room smelled of Alana. Lilac and vanilla, he realized, spying the small bottles of lotion on her dresser. And then his gaze fell to her bed.

"Christ," he muttered.

Lying across the neatly tucked comforter was a black nightie. A barely there slip of material that he imagined wouldn't cover much.

He forced himself toward the adjoining bathroom and then the walk-in closet. Both were clear. He'd just faced that damn bed when a voice came from the recesses of the hallway.

"Did you find anything?"

"Jesus!" Chandler whirled around, shoving the gun in the holster along his back. "Didn't I tell you to wait outside?"

She ignored that question as she peeked her head into the bedroom. "Did you?"

Walking past her, he caught her by the arm and ushered her back into the living room. "Did you leave the lights on?"

44

"Yes." She wrenched her arm free in a move so dramatic, he wondered how she didn't yank her own arm out of its socket. "So, there's nothing out of place?"

"You tell me." He watched her look around, totally picturing her in that nightie. Yep. His cock was hard again.

"Everything looks fine to me," she said.

Her lips pursed, and then she stalked off down the hallway. He lingered for a moment and then followed her, finding her standing before a medium-size oak desk. The file was still clenched in one hand, and she was holding a pad of stationary in the other as she faced him.

"See," she said, and gestured as though she were holding the shredded files from Watergate. Her glasses were slightly askew on her nose. The urge to fix them came out of nowhere, and what the fuck was up with that? "This is my stationary. I had it specially made," she added.

Wondering who actually took the time to get personalized stationary made, he pulled out the note and unfolded it. It was definitely a match. The word was written in childish, blockish handwriting.

His eyes met hers. Part of him wanted to tell her that it could be coincidental. Obviously he hoped that was the case. Even though Chad believed that the publicist was the antichrist, Chandler didn't like the idea of this being anything more than a harmless, run-of-the-mill lunatic.

But he was a logical man. Unless Alana wrote the note and threw the rock through her own windshield, someone had slipped into her apartment at some point and retrieved the stationary from her desk.

That had to be taken seriously.

Alana fixed her glasses, her bottom lip trembling as she spoke. "Someone's been in my apartment."

His chest tightened as real fear snaked up his spine. "I think it's time that I look at those letters."

So many different emotions swirled through Alana as she sat in her living room, watching Chandler pore over the letters in her kitchen. Anger. Frustration. Fear. They mingled together, causing her to go from furious to terrified in seconds and giving her one fierce headache.

Someone had been in her apartment.

Her heart dropped at the thought. When? While she had left to go find Chandler or before then? How many days could've passed and she'd never known? Better yet, how had someone gotten *into* her apartment?

"How long have you been receiving these?" Chandler asked, drawing her attention.

She took off her glasses, placing them onto the bar. The clock on the stove said it was after midnight and her eyes felt full of grit. "For about a year."

"Any idea who it could be? An ex-boyfriend?"

A dry laugh escaped. "No."

"You've never had an ex-boyfriend?"

"Not anyone in the last couple of years who hates my guts." The look of disbelief on his striking face irked her. "All my breakups have been amicable."

"Husbands?"

"No," she said.

"Girlfriends?"

She rolled her eyes.

46

A brief grin appeared, and she was surprised to see it. Something about it told her that a lot of people probably lived their whole lives without seeing that grin. "What about clients?"

Rubbing her temples, she shook her head. "There have been people . . . *upset* with me in the past."

Chandler snorted.

Lifting her lashes, she felt a nasty retort forming on the tip of her tongue, mostly out of habit, but it died off before she could open her mouth. Their gazes locked, and she could easily recall how much Chad had loathed her existence. No doubt Chandler felt the same out of association. It bothered her.

"I'm not a terrible person," she said, her voice low. "I know that's hard to believe."

He blinked. "I didn't say you were."

"I take my job seriously," she continued, drawing in a shallow breath. When she spoke again, her voice was hoarse. "I've built a—a *stellar* reputation in a very short time. And if that means I have to make people do what they don't want to do and they'll hate me for it, so be it. But in the end, everyone—*everyone*—is in a better position after I leave them."

Something flickered across his face, and then he looked away, a muscle working along his jaw. "Obviously someone doesn't feel that way."

An old, familiar ache pierced her chest at those words. Alana loved her job and it meant everything to her, but sometimes it required her to do things she didn't want. During her short career, she had hurt and used people.

47

Most thought she was apathetic about it all, but that was the furthest from the truth. The things she had to do kept her awake at night. As a publicist, there were times when she had to climb into the muck and drag her clients out of it, ensuring that they came out all shiny. That wasn't easy. And some of her clients didn't want to be dragged out.

Looking at Chandler, she knew in the deepest recesses of her soul this was something she probably had in common with him. He looked like there were dark things in his past, things he had to do—didn't regret, but wished he hadn't had to.

Regret and wishing for something else were two very different things.

"The best thing you can do is write down a list of people you think have a reason to go this far." He gathered up the letters, placing them in the file. "I can run some background checks once you get the list. Mind if I keep these?"

"So does this mean you're going to work for me?"

He stared at her. "First off, I don't work for anyone."

She needed a strong drink to deal with him. "Okay. Wrong word choice or whatever, but I need more than a few background checks done. I've accepted a job with a local firm that works with politicians and companies—"

"Basically doing damage control?" he asked, sounding genuinely curious.

"That's one way to look at it, but it's more than that. It's working with media, scheduling events, and prepping for interviews and preventing a problem before it occurs." Excitement thrummed through her, and she sat a little straighter. "It's a huge opportunity. I won't have to do as much traveling or dealing with so many, well, crazy people. No offense, but playing babysitter to people like your brother wasn't nearly as fun as you'd think it was."

"No offense taken," he commented drily.

"Anyway, I can't have anything interfering with this position. There's absolutely nothing worse than a publicist with drama. Plus, I'm going to be around important individuals, and I can't put them in danger if this asshole tries something. I need someone who can blend in when I'm in public, just in case, and can be discreet. No one can know about this."

Dropping his elbows onto the counter, he leaned forward. "Hiring a member of CCG Security isn't cheap, Alana. You're talking after hours, which is double, and travel if necessary."

"I know and . . . and I've made good money. I can afford you." She curled her hands into fists, moving them into her lap. She hated being in this situation, having to rely on someone. It had been many years since she'd had to. "So are you going to take the job?"

Chandler's deep-blue gaze turned thoughtful. "Write down the list of people and let me check out a few things first."

That wasn't the answer she was looking for. Irritation flushed her skin, but she fought the urge to demand a yes or no.

He must've sensed her frustration because his lips tipped up at the corners. "Look, you may not need to hire someone. If we can track down who it is, all it may take is a phone call to scare him off. Nine out of ten times, people pull this kind of shit because they think they won't be confronted. They hide behind bullshit."

Hope sparked in her chest. "Even people who vandalize cars and break into apartments?"

"Yes."

She wanted to believe that more than anything. It would make things so much easier. "Even someone who's followed me clear across the country?"

"You don't know if the person followed you. He could be out here on business or whatever. And it's easier than you think to find someone's address. Actually, you probably know that."

She lowered her gaze as the unspoken words hung between them. She did know how easy it was. After all, she'd tracked down Bridget by paying a few dollars to an online website. All it took was one utility in someone's name, and bam, address and any other personal information was right at your fingertips.

Before, she had never really considered how someone would feel or realized how incredibly creepy it was when she pulled that crap.

"I'm a creeper," she muttered.

"What?" He laughed.

Shaking her head, she leaned over and grabbed a notepad and pen. "Nothing. Give me a few minutes and I'll give you a list."

She could feel his eyes on her as she started scribbling down names of former clients and their associates who could potentially have a beef with her. There was Michelle Ward—a pro tennis player who had gotten addicted to painkillers after a knee injury. Alana practically had the girl kidnapped and dropped into rehab under the ruse of visiting a new health spa. Even though Michelle was off drugs and back playing professionally again, she had never gotten over it.

Then there was Jennifer Van Gunten—an actress whose hard-partying ways and bad-news boyfriend had nearly destroyed her career. The insurance the production companies had to take out on her for any of her roles was astronomical and the first thing Alana had to do was end the young actress's ties with her boyfriend and friends. She doubted it was any of them, since the crowd Jennifer had run with was made up of all spoiled rich kids who probably moved on quickly, but she scribbled their names down anyway—namely Brent King, the on and off again boyfriend slash small time dealer. The few run ins she'd had with him in the past had not been pretty. The guy had an anger problem. Once, when she had to pull Jennifer out of a club that night before a court appearance, Brent had taken a swing at her, and she vaguely remembered him having some ties to the D.C. area. But again, he was a spoiled rich kid. She doubted he even remembered her.

There was William Manafee—a football player whose off-the-field practices, much like Chad's, had started to gain more press than his ability to play ball. The big difference was that William had been married and, while his wife had mostly been in the dark, Alana had used his wife as leverage. William had cleaned himself up, but his wife had overheard one of their conversations, and now his monthly alimony was as much as her yearly salary. He blamed Alana for his inability to keep his dick in his pants.

There were a few more clients she had worked with who might carry a grudge for one reason or another, and she quickly scribbled each name on the paper. She was almost finished when she decided to add one more name, and then slid the sheet of paper toward Chandler.

He scanned the names, and she knew the moment he got to the end, because his brows shot up. He looked at her through his lashes. "Chad Gamble?"

Her lips twitched as she shrugged. "He wasn't very happy with me."

One brow continued to rise.

She fought off a giggle. "I was just joking."

"I'd hope so. Would really be awkward if it were him." He winked.

Her lips split into a small smile as she imagined Christmas dinners going forward if that were the case. Then she laughed as her gaze dropped to where his fingers rested on the edge of the paper. "Sorry. Just picturing that conversation."

When there was no response, she lifted her gaze and found him watching her intently. So much so that she wondered if she had done something wrong. Holding eye contact with those clear eyes wasn't easy. Chandler's intensity could be intimidating, and he stared at her as if he could see right into her.

Then his gaze dropped to her mouth, and she felt her lips part on a soft inhale. She was easily reminded of how he'd felt pressed against her in the parking lot. A heaviness filled her breasts, an almost sweet aching.

"Do you have anyone you can stay with?" he asked,

pushing off the counter and slipping her paper into his pocket.

Alana almost laughed again, except it wasn't funny. She had no one. "I thought there was a good chance this person wouldn't be too much of a threat."

"So I'm guessing you don't have anyone you can stay with," he replied instead, horrifically astute.

She felt her cheeks burn and immediately went on the defensive, which ended in her lying. "I have someone I can stay with."

His eyes narrowed. "Then you should probably do that. Just in case. You shouldn't be staying here." He started around the counter and then stopped. "Do you need a ride or anything to your friend's place? I can wait."

Surprised by the fact that he was being so helpful, it took her a second to respond. "No. I'll call him in a few. It's late, and I don't want to be any more inconvenient than I've been."

His jaw clenched. "You haven't been inconvenient."

She laughed as she slid off the barstool. "You're a terrible liar. I interrupted what was probably going to be a very interesting night for you." The moment those words came out of her mouth, an irrational prick of jealousy burned in her stomach. "Wait here. I'll get you my card."

When she returned from the office, she saw he'd placed a card of his own on the counter. She handed hers over. "How much will I owe you to run the background checks and do some digging?"

He stopped at the door, head cocked to the side. "Who is the 'he' you're staying with?"

At first, she didn't get what he meant. "A friend."

"A friend like Paula?" he asked.

Instead of answering the question, she smiled. "What do I owe you for this?"

Stepping out in the quiet hallway, Chandler faced her. "Let me drop you off at your friend's house."

Uh, no. That was not going to happen. "That's not necessary, but thank you."

"It's no trouble."

Her spine stiffened. "I didn't say it was any trouble to you, but it's not necessary."

He stared at her for a long moment. "I mean it, Alana. Don't stay in this apartment."

Alana shifted her weight from one foot to the other. Staying here would be stupid. Frankly, the idea of being in the apartment alone right now, knowing that someone had been here, creeped her out. She was going to have to check into a hotel. "I'm not."

His head tilted slightly. Through the layers of her starched and stiff clothing, she felt his stare move from the tips of her shoes to the top of her head. His lips curved up as his gaze locked with hers. "I'll get back to you on that, Miss Gore."

After Chandler left, Alana quickly gathered up a day or two's worth of clothing and some personal stuff. She packed it up neatly and exited the apartment after calling for a cab.

She'd claimed earlier she hadn't been a terrible person, but that wasn't entirely honest. Of course, she wasn't a great person, either.

Paranoia kept causing her to look over her shoulder in the brightly lit lobby as she waited for the cab to arrive. She ended up checking into a hotel within walking distance of her office.

It wasn't a bad hotel but definitely not a four-star. The place carried a faint scent of musk, but it was the best she could do in the middle of the night.

Ten minutes later she was checked into a room on the second level that was unfortunately not far enough from the bar. She closed the door behind her, threw the deadbolt, and rolled her suitcase to the bed. Looking around the small room, the queen-size bed with small, square pillows and the generic desk next to a TV, she let out a deep sigh. The muffled conversation and laughter made it through the thick walls, traveling from the bar down the hall.

For some reason, hearing that—hearing people happy and laughing and living—while she was standing in a hotel room that smelled of . . . of burned matches, got to her.

She plopped down on the bed, wishing she'd had the foresight to grab a carton of ice cream from her freezer. It felt like it was going to be one of those "look at your life, look at your choices" kinds of night, and she needed chocolate to deal with that shit.

Feeling more alone than she had in many years, she scooted back across the uncomfortable bed and tucked her knees against her chest. She sighed, dropping her chin on her knees. It was going to be a long night.

Chapter Five

At his office two days later, Chandler scrolled through the results on the names Alana had given him for a third time. He wasn't sure what, if anything, he would find. These things were like puzzles and it never helped when the person in need of his assistance lied.

Staying with a friend.

Bullshit.

After leaving her apartment, he'd driven around the block and then parked down the street from her apartment. Thirty minutes later and just when he was about to go right back up to that apartment and drag her ass out of it, a cab showed up and out came Alana, tugging along a small suitcase.

What kind of male would let her take a cab to his house at this time of night? he'd wondered, but then he had his answer shortly thereafter.

He hadn't believed it at first. Alana hadn't gone to a friend's house. Nope. She'd checked into a hotel. Not even an extremely great one, either.

Jesus.

How could she have absolutely no one here? And if

there was not a single person who could help her out in a time of need, why in the hell did she move to this city? She was truly all alone, and something about that didn't sit well.

Still didn't sit well with him two days later.

He'd almost gone into the hotel room that night, but what would he have done? Taken her back to his house? Frankly, the woman had too much pride for that, so he let it go and tailed her ass the following morning, early enough to catch her before she left for work.

She'd actually *walked* to work.

And then she'd walked back to the hotel later that evening. Alone. With a potential stalker watching her. Nice.

The bad thing was, he'd actually been relieved that she wasn't staying with some tool. He rolled his eyes. There was a lot wrong with that.

It was going to take a little more digging, given that most of the suspects were public figures. What he got wasn't much. Only Michelle Ward had any contact information, and he'd fielded a return call from her this morning.

The tennis player was most definitely not a fan of Miss Gore, but his instincts were telling him that she didn't have anything to do with this threat. And if anything, the Ward chick was reluctantly grateful for Miss Gore's interference and tactics.

Just like his brother.

When Alana had talked about her job, it was obvious the woman took it seriously and it meant something to her. It was also obvious that the way some of her clients viewed her got to her, which surprised him. From his

57

previous run-ins with her, he'd thought she had bigger balls than he did.

His gaze moved to the note that had been wrapped around the brick. Could someone else have the same kind of specialized stationary? It was more than just possible, but the likelihood of the person using the stationary and not knowing that Alana had the same was as likely as a UFO landing on the Washington Monument.

He briefly entertained the idea of calling her and checking in, but she hadn't called him. And he really didn't have a reason to be calling her other than . . .

Well, other than hearing her voice, and if he called her for that reason, then he'd grown a vagina at some point.

"Joe's Body Shop called. You know, just in case you were wondering why the phone was ringing off the fucking hook."

He shifted at the sound of Murray's voice. The man was leaning against the doorframe, arms folded. Murray was Chase's age but had the attitude of a crotchety old man half the time.

Murray limped into the office and plopped down in the chair across from Chandler's desk. "So when did you get a Lexus? Thought you were a live-and-die Ford redneck?"

He took a sip of his coffee. "It's not mine."

"Then who has someone so pissed off at them that thousands of dollars of damage was done to their car?" He ran a hand over his close-shaven skull, the fingers brushing tattoos running up and down his neck and throat. Murray could be one scary motherfucker if you met him in a dark alley. "I thought only you pissed off people that badly."

Grinning, Chandler sat his cup down. "Nope. Apparently there are people out there who have a more charming personality than I do."

Murray snorted. "Working on a new case?" When Chandler didn't say anything, the other man was used to it. "What're the details? Because I'm curious. You got William-mother fucking-Manafee's name written down."

Seeing no way of getting Murray out of his office without giving him the lowdown, Chandler told him about the possible case, quick and to the point.

"Shit." Murray sat back, scrubbing at the stubble on his face. "You're talking about Chad's publicist?"

He nodded.

A slow grin appeared as Murray dropped his hand onto the arm of the chair. "Is that his name on the list of suspects?"

"Yep."

"Awesome." Murray laughed. "You think the douche behind this is serious?"

"Don't know." He flicked his gaze to the screen. "I've only been able to get ahold of one person and rule her out. Alana is a ball breaker—no doubt about it—but is this person serious? Hard to believe."

"Alana? First-name basis?"

"Shut up," he said, kicking his booted feet up on the desk. "And you know, even though her tactics may piss off people, she repairs their images, ultimately leaves them in a better situation than they were in before. How can you seriously hate someone who does that for you enough to want to hurt her?"

"Are you sure it's a client, then?" he asked, his dark eyes

sparking with the interest of a new case and all its wonderful, fucked-up possibilities.

"Could be an ex. I know she said she doesn't have any, but you know just as well as I do, sometimes it takes the question to be asked a time or two to get a straight answer." But he didn't think Alana had lied about that. The woman had been rattled when she'd seen the note. He doubted she'd hide important info, like a psychotic ex-boyfriend, from him.

"So you've been tailing her?"

He nodded. "She's at work right now."

"Want me to see if I can track down some of the numbers? I got a friend who's a friend of a player on the Falcons. And obviously I can't do nothing else but sit behind a desk."

Chandler laughed as he pushed the list over. "Who do you know?"

"Remember the Redskins cheerleader two years ago? The one who was being stalked by that parolee? Well, we've stayed in contact. I'm sure she can make a few calls and point us in the right direction."

He shook his head. "Yeah, I bet the contact you've been staying in has been totally professional and doesn't involve your cock."

"I am not talking to you about my cock."

Chandler's eyes narrowed. "Do I need to remind you of the number-one rule?"

"Whatever." Murray pushed himself up. "Do I need to remind *you* about the rule?"

"Shut the fuck up."

Murray laughed as he ambled out of the office, closing

the door behind him. Looking back at the screen, Chandler let about five seconds go by before his gaze fell to the small card propped along his keyboard. He thought about the nightie that had been lying on Alana's bed, and his jeans tightened.

Chandler knew the rules. He'd fucking written them.

He just didn't always follow them.

Besides, he hadn't technically been hired by Miss Gore, so what the fuck ever.

Picking up the card, a slow smile spread across his face. He wanted to say that it would've made a difference if she had hired him, but Chandler hadn't made a habit of lying to himself before.

Why start now?

There was something about Little Miss Alana Gore that got to him, crawled under his skin, and had him acting worse than Chase and Chad combined. He didn't know what it was or what it would mean, but he would find out.

Because unlike his brothers, when he wanted something, he didn't fuck around and neither did he spend time bullshitting himself. When Chandler wanted something, he went right for it.

And he wanted Alana.

Every time Alana walked into her office at Images, she was reminded of exactly where she came from. What she had to overcome to get to where she was now. If Granny were still alive, she would've been proud—bitter as all hell, but she would've been proud.

Smoothing her hand across the polished oak desk, she

inhaled deeply and let it out slowly. Nothing was going to screw this up.

The door to her office flew open and Ruby Baker stormed in, her blond hair sticking out at the temples. Her partner at the publicist firm was only a few years older than she was and had reminded Alana of a librarian, with her collared shirts and pressed linen pants. "We have a problem."

Alana stiffened behind the desk. "What?"

"End-of-the-world scenario," she said. Closing the door behind her, she leaned against it. "We just got a call from a journalist at the *Washington Post*, inquiring about Dick in A Box."

Her eyes widened as her stomach dropped. Okay. That could screw this up. She smacked her hands down on the edge of her desk. "How?"

"I don't know." Ruby strolled forward, slumped in the chair, and threw her arms up. "Everyone who knows about this has been either paid off, warned off, or suddenly sent off vacationing in the sunny tropics of Jamaica."

"Someone had to have said something." Alana cursed under her breath as she mentally sprinted through all those involved in the latest shenanigans. "I bet you it's the maid. I told you she was going to be a problem. She has two kids she wants to put into private school. There's money in this story."

Ruby groaned.

Damn senators and their dicks all the way to hell and back.

Every publicist's nightmare was getting saddled with a

horny politician who had no control over what hung between his legs. Of course, Alana had been assigned to Senator Grant, along with Ruby and the last publicist. Key word being *last*, as in no longer worked for Images. This senator had been around the block a time or two when it came to scandalous activity.

Alana was a firm believer in the fact God and the Holy Ghost hated her.

Apparently the name Dick in A Box had came about two years ago, when the senator had his junk out underneath a FedEx box, giving one of his fake secretaries easy access. Someone in the office had played the *Saturday Night Live* skit and the name stuck.

"The reporter was asking about the call girl." As Ruby continued, Alana swore wispy strands of hair further escaped the woman's bun. "I deterred him, made up some bullshit lie about the senator hiring new staff for his house, but . . ."

"But now the *Post* will be watching him. Great. We need to talk to the senator." Sighing, she felt like face-planting into the desk. "Rock. Paper. Scissors?"

A grin appeared on the woman's face. "On the count of three."

Alana had gone with paper. Ruby had picked scissors. It was official. The entire Holy Trinity hated her. She pushed back in her chair and bent, reaching for her purse.

Her phone rang, causing her to jump. There was no number on the caller ID, so it had to be an outside number. Picking up the receiver, she watched Ruby slide farther down in her seat. "Images. This is Alana Gore."

"I prefer Miss Gore. Sounds like you want to punish someone when you say it."

Holy shit. It was Chandler. She didn't know about her punishing him, but she could totally picture him punishing *her*. Her cheeks felt hot, and across from her, curiosity marked Ruby's face.

The gap of silence stretched out obnoxiously. "Alana, are you there?"

"Yes. I'm here. Sorry," she blurted out, blinking several times. "You, uh, caught me off guard." She wished she were alone, because he had to have discovered something. "What can I help you with?"

"You."

"Me?"

"Yes," he replied, voice low and smooth. "I want you."

Her mouth rounded. He wanted her?

A deep chuckle sent a shiver down her spine. "You haven't had lunch yet."

For a moment, his words didn't process, and then they did. How did he know she hadn't had lunch? Her eyes darted to the clock on her monitor. "It's three in the afternoon."

"Some people have a late lunch."

Painfully aware Ruby was listening, she tightened her fingers around the phone. "Already had lunch."

"Liar," came the quick reply. "So, what about dinner?"

Why in the hell was he asking her about dinner now? "Did you find anything out about what you're looking into?"

"You didn't answer my question."

Smothering a ripe curse, she smiled tightly at Ruby and then twisted sideways in her chair. "I will probably be working late tonight. And as you know, I'm at work right now, so I really shouldn't be on the phone."

"I'm at work and I'm on the phone."

She squeezed her eyes shut as she bent over and reached for her purse again. "Well, you own your business. I do not."

"True," he replied, and then she heard him make a sound that had her stomach tightening. Was he stretching? Touching himself? "I spoke with Michelle Ward. She's not the culprit. Still looking into it."

She was totally picturing him touching himself now. Hand in his unbuttoned jeans, no shirt—he couldn't be wearing a shirt in her fantasy—and his hand around his thickness, slowly stroking himself. A sharp pulse pounded between her thighs. Like a match thrown to gasoline, her body sparked alive. Her response startled her.

It also sort of thrilled her.

"Alana?" The way he said her name was as though he was tasting it on his tongue. "Did you hang up on me?"

"No. I'm just busy." Busy picturing him masturbating. Her brain really needed to work itself out. She sat up, and once Ruby saw her face, her coworker frowned. "Thanks for the update. I'll have to call you later."

"I'll call you."

With that, there was a distinctive *click* and Chandler was gone. She slowly placed the phone back on the receiver.

"Who was that?"

She debated lying, but if he ended up working for her,

65

she was going to be seen with him. Might as well get it out there now. "Chandler Gamble."

Ruby nearly came out of her seat. "As in Chad Gamble's brother, right?"

She nodded as she stood. "You know I worked with his brother a few months ago."

"It's what got you the job here." Ruby stood, her green eyes twinkling. "So what were you doing talking lunch plans with *him*?"

The way Ruby said "him" made her uneasy. She headed for the door. "I ran into him a few days ago, when I had car trouble, and he helped me out."

"But that doesn't explain lunch or dinner or why your face was red through the whole call." Ruby ducked her, blocking the exit. "Are you seeing Chandler?"

Alana laughed. "No. We're friends." The word sounded lame even to her ears.

"Are you telling me the truth?"

Her brows pinched. "Yes. I'm telling you the truth."

"Chandler is hot shit, and the things they say about him and what he likes to do?" She fanned herself as she tugged on her collar. "I wouldn't kick him out of my bed for eating crackers, and I'm happily married."

Her body quivered. She'd heard some of the things Chandler liked to do. Hell, she'd seen some of those things about to happen at Leather and Lace.

"So how well do you know him?" she asked.

Alana searched for patience. "Not really well. Like I said, we sort of ran into each other."

"When you were having car problems? Tell me, when

you were working with Chad, you had to have gotten the details on Chandler. Is it true? The stuff they say? That he goes to Leather and Lace and is into dominance and some really crazy sex?"

Her mouth opened, but she snapped it shut. From all she had gathered when she'd been working with Chad and from what she'd seen with her own two eyes, everything pointed toward an affirmative. Part of her was seconds away from divulging what she knew. After all, part of being a publicist was being on top of all the gossip, but something inside wouldn't let her.

His sex life was definitely not her or Ruby's business. "I think all of that is just rumors," she said finally, smiling. "There was nothing I found that suggested it's true."

Ruby's face fell. "Well, that sucks. I was hoping you were going to hook up with him and I could live vicariously through you and experience some freaky sex."

Her lips pursed. "Sorry to disappoint?"

"Oh well. Go give the senator hell."

Saying good-bye, Alana headed out of the office and to the rental car she'd picked up yesterday. An interesting realization poked at her as she threw her purse onto the passenger's seat. She should be focused on what she was going to say to the senator, but all she was really thinking about was how she was going to indulge in her earlier fantasy later tonight.

Before she headed out to the senator's, she swung by the coffee shop down the block, in need of caffeine fortitude if she was going to make it. The line was short, and as she stepped in the back, she checked the time on her cell.

When it was her turn, she smiled at the young girl behind the counter. "French Vanilla, easy on—"

"The cream," interrupted a familiar voice from behind her.

"Yes. That's right." She turned, surprised, and then gaped. "Steven?"

The man behind her smiled, crinkling the skin behind his glasses and flashing a set of perfect white teeth. "Hello, Alana."

"Hey, what are you doing out on the east coast?" She stepped to the side as the cashier fulfilled her order, somewhat dumbfounded by seeing Steven Grimes in a coffee shop in D.C. "Work?"

He nodded, shoving his hand into the pocket's of his pressed pants. "You know me, bouncing back and forth."

Not really expecting to have seen him again, she forced a smile as she struggled for something to say and hoped her order was filled quickly. "So, how have you been?"

"Busy?" he said, his gaze dipping over her. "How have you been? You're looking great."

"So are you," she mumbled, turning as her coffee was handed over. "I've been busy, too. I'm actually running late to see a client." She started to back away. "But it's really good seeing you. We should do dinner sometime." She had absolutely no plans of doing that, but it sounded polite.

Steven's smile spread. "I'd love that. I'm actually engaged now. Would love for you to meet her."

"Oh." Well, shit, was everyone getting married? "That's really nice. Congratulations."

"Thank you," he replied. "You?"

Me? Ah, yes, here comes the awkward moment. "There's . . . um, no one I'm too serious with." As in no one in general, but he didn't need to know that. "Well, then I'll call you." She was almost to the door. "It's nice seeing you."

Alana ducked out before she had to make any more embarrassingly stilted conversation.

God, she was the most awkward person ever when it came to running into exes. As cruel as it sounded, she was the type of person who, when the relationship was over for her, was done and could live happily ever after if she never ran into him again.

Steven was a blast from the past, a man who'd claimed to love her, and while she'd cared for him deeply, it hadn't worked out. He'd wanted more, a part of her that Alana had never been able to give. That had saddened her, still did. Steven would've made the perfect husband—successful doctor, well traveled with homes on the east and west coast, patient, and alarmingly kind.

But after a few months, Alana had grown restless and had sensed that Steven would continue to push for more from her: a serious commitment, and that wasn't what she wanted. He'd been upset when she broke off the relationship at the beginning of last year, claiming that she was running from him and her feelings.

She was happy to hear he was engaged, though. He was a good man and deserved a rich, happy life.

It didn't take too long to shake off the weirdness from the unexpected meeting, but as she walked back to her office's parking a garage, she shivered. The feeling of . . . of being watched was so strong, she looked over her shoulder, but all she saw was a sea of unfamiliar faces.

The odd sensation stayed with her until she climbed into her rental car. It could be paranoia or something else, but how could she tell the difference? All she could do was be vigilant.

After about an hour drive to make it out to the senator's home in Alexandria, she discovered the senator half dressed with yet another woman of questionable employment right in his foyer, while his wife was at a charity function.

The man had no impulse control.

It took her an ugly amount of time to explain why fornication with prostitutes shouldn't be high on his to-do list, and then nearly two hours to get back into the city due to a traffic snarl on the beltway. By the time she pulled into the parking garage, all she wanted to do was eat her weight in pie and call it a night. At least it was Friday night. As long as her senator didn't run through his gated community naked, she could grab what she needed from her apartment and head back to the hotel, order room service, and hole up like a sloth.

Chandler hadn't called her back. She could've called him, and she almost did on the way to her apartment. The idea of going there alone gave her the creeps, but she couldn't bring herself to press the numbers into her cell. He'd said he would call her. Calling him seemed... It seemed what? Like she was interested in something other than what she had come to him for?

She rode the elevator up to her floor, chewing on the inside of her cheek. Although she'd been expecting a call from him, it had completely caught her off guard. Well, her reaction to his call was what truly surprised her. The rest of the afternoon and well into the evening, she'd experienced alternating flashes of edgy excitement and then queasy nervousness. It had felt like forever since she'd been attracted to someone or felt like a giddy girl with a secret crush.

And she was far from being a giddy girl.

Walking to her door, she dug her keys out of her bag as her thoughts spun around the possibility that she was actually harboring a godforsaken *crush* on Chandler Gamble. Of all the eligible men she came into contact with on a daily basis, her body would have to decide it was*him* it was interested in. He was the worst possible choice, considering his wild reputation. Normally Alana gravitated toward the quiet and safe men, the kind whose good time consisted of movies and takeout. Not whips, handcuffs, and God knows what else Chandler brought to the table, but there was something about him that made her want to let loose and . . . and get a little wild.

Alana had never been wild. Not once in her entire life, which was amazing given the genes she'd inherited. None of her relationships had ever evoked the nervous rush of excitement or the kind of attraction that had her catching her breath. But it was better like that. Way too many women in her family had fallen prey to lust that flipped into unrequited love that destroyed the potential of their lives.

So caught up in her thoughts, she almost didn't notice that her door was ajar as she reached forward to slide in the key. Her breath caught and the tiny hairs on the back of her neck rose.

71

Time slowed down as her instincts fired off warnings, telling her to get the hell out of there, to call the police, but she saw her hand, incredibly pale and trembling, push open the door.

What she saw wrenched a horrified cry from deep inside her chest and almost brought her to her knees.

Chapter Six

"Chad is such a pansy ass."

Sitting next to his brother on the large sofa, Chandler snorted as he nursed a beer. He and Chase were watching Chad on the big screen, pitching against the Braves. The Nationals were in the fifth inning, likely to win big in the away game.

The camera zoomed in on Chad as he lifted his left leg and reared back, prepared to deliver another wicked fastball. From this angle, it was hard not to notice the fuchsia hanky tucked in the back pocket of his uniform—his Bridget-inspired good luck charm and what, according to Chase, made him a pansy ass.

"Look who's talking," Chandler replied mildly, taking a swig of his beer. "I think you broke the record for how many texts you can send a girlfriend in an hour."

Chase shot him a look. "Whatever. Maddie isn't feeling well, so I'm checking in on her."

Real concern pinched his features as he looked at his brother. Maddie was like a little sister to Chandler and he cared for her deeply. "What's wrong with her?

"I think she's got the flu," he said, his gaze moving from

73

the screen to his phone. "Woke up this morning throwing up like she was on an all-night bender. I told her I'd stay home with her tonight, but she told me to leave or she'd kick my ass."

Chandler's lips twitched into a smile. "You're not going to the clubs tonight, then?"

"Hell no." Chase had taken over their father's business, running and operating several exclusive clubs throughout the tri-state area. "I'm already itching to get back to her, so I'm sure as hell not going to spend half the night away just in case she gets sicker."

"Then you should be home."

Chase glanced at him. "Like I said, she threatened to kick my ass. You know how she gets."

He laughed. Maddie was a tiny thing, but he wouldn't put it past her to make good on her threat. "You should pick her up some ginger ale and crackers."

"Yes, Mom."

Chandler flipped him off as he kicked his leg off the coffee table and leaned back. A foul ball cracked up into the air, then got snatched by the catcher, ending the inning. As it switched to a commercial, his thoughts wandered to the phone call he'd made earlier and a small grin pulled at his lips.

He'd flustered the un-fluster-able and didn't that fill him with a ridiculous amount of smugness? He really shouldn't be messing with her, considering the situation she was in, but he just couldn't help himself.

His own phone sat like a stone on the arm of the sofa. He hadn't expected Alana to call him, even if she'd said that she would. It wasn't like her, but damn if he wasn't seconds away from turning into Chase. He wanted her, and he knew she wasn't going to make it easy, but he needed to proceed with caution. He had a feeling that the more he pushed, the more she'd push back. And while her snappy mouth and fierce personality were a huge part of her allure, he didn't want her to close him out before he even got in.

But maybe . . . maybe he'd swing by her hotel later, accidentally, of course.

"Did you get fitted for your tux yet?" Chase asked, throwing his arm along the back of the couch. "Please tell me I'm not the only one who hasn't. I'm pretty sure Mitch got it done already."

"No." Chandler laughed. "The wedding's not until June. We have plenty of time—"

A knock on his front door interrupted him. He started to move, but Chase got up, sliding his phone into his pocket. "I'll see who it is."

"Have at it." Chandler leaned back as Chase disappeared from the room.

He wasn't expecting anyone, but it could be Murray or one of the other guys who worked for him. But when his brother returned, rocking one hell of a "what the fuck" expression, he knew it couldn't be one of them.

"You have a guest."

"No shit," Chandler replied drily. "Where is said guest?"

Chase eyed him strangely. "Where I left her—inside the foyer."

Her? Chandler dropped his feet to the floor in surprise.

75

Before Chase even continued, he already had a suspicion of who it could be.

"Do I even want to know why Chad's publicist is here?" Chase demanded in a low voice.

"Ex," he muttered, putting his beer down on the coffee table.

Chase made a face. "Like the fact that she no longer works for Chad matters. What the hell . . . ?"

Whatever else his brother was saying was lost to him. Chandler left him standing in the living room as he made his way through the dining room. Curiosity was riding him hard. Alana had sought him out? Not even calling him, but coming to his house? Fuck yeah. Maybe this wouldn't be as hard as he thought.

His curiosity turned to apprehension the moment he laid eyes on her.

Alana stood with her back plastered to his front door, holding a black purse to her chest in the same manner she'd held the file folder. Tiny strands of raven-colored hair wisped around a face that was way too pale. She was in another boxy, lackluster suit that seemed to swallow her whole. Her eyes were impossibly wide, the look about them wounded and scared.

"Are you okay?" he demanded, his voice harsher than he intended.

She flinched and croaked out, "I'm sorry. I didn't know where else to go."

"Sorry for what?" He made sure his voice was softer this time as he approached her. "What happened?"

Her lower lip trembled as she swallowed hard. "I went

home after work to get a few things and discovered that someone had broken into my apartment."

"Shit," he muttered, thrusting a hand through his hair. He would've tailed her ass this evening, but watching Chad on the big screen was tradition. The muscles in the back of his neck tensed. "But you're okay?"

She gave a quick jerk of her chin, but her face was still too pale. "I should've called, but—"

"No. It's okay. Did you call the police?" When she nodded, he cursed again. "Did they just take a report?"

"Yes. I told them about the letters and my car, but there's really nothing they could do at the moment and I couldn't—"

"Go back to the hotel?"

She blinked. "How ... how did you ...? Of course," she said numbly. "You've been watching me."

"I've been keeping an eye on you. There's a difference."

Several moments passed as she seemed to let that sink in. "I didn't know what to do." She drew in a deep breath that shuddered through her frame. "I don't have anyone else ..." She trailed off, clamping her lips tightly together and shaking her head.

"Fuck, Alana. I told you not to stay in your apartment. You could've been home when—"

"I know. I'm sorry, but I didn't want to ..."

Admit that there wasn't anyone she could go to. Shaking his head, he looked away for a second. Truth was, she could've just been honest, but she was too damn stubborn for that.

"Are you sure you're okay? No one was there when you showed up?"

She shook her head.

Apprehension flipped to anger in less than a second. Partly due to the fact that someone had been in her apartment again and also partly toward himself. He should've fucking tailed her tonight.

Alana drew in a shallow breath, drawing his stare. "Everything was destroyed, Chandler—my couch, curtains, furniture, and clothes. Food was pulled out of the fridge, emptied all over the floors and my bed." She broke off suddenly, her eyes blinking furiously. "*Everything*. Looked like someone took a knife to it. I have rental insurance, but to do all that? And the letters—I left them in the file on my desk. They were gone."

At the sight of her valiantly holding back tears, something unhinged in his chest. Alana was strong and stubborn, but through the course of his career, he'd seen people break over less things. Having her home broken into repeatedly and having her personal items destroyed was enough to put anyone in shock, especially someone like Alana, who would try to control the path of a tornado.

Something like this sent a clear message: the perpetrator was the only one in control. It also said that the person had moved beyond harmless threats. Someone wanted to scare Alana badly enough to send her running, something he doubted she did often, and he'd succeeded.

The woman looked like her legs would give out on her at any moment. The urge to take her into his arms hit him hard. He wanted to hold her. More than that, he wanted to protect her. That sudden need went beyond his job, but he resisted. Something told him that she would most likely

78

react like a wild animal cornered if he did pull her into an embrace.

"Come on," he said quietly. Taking her arm in a gentle grasp, he led her into the living room so she could sit.

His brother's brows nearly reached his hair as he watched Chandler guide a quiet Alana to the edge of the couch. She tucked her hands between her knees, but he could still see them trembling.

A feeling of helplessness assaulted him, a sensation he wasn't used to at all. Chandler knew how to protect people. He made a living doing it, but so far, he'd done a piss-poor job of doing so.

Turning to his brother, he curled his hands into fists. "Can you go get us a glass of whiskey?"

Chase opened his mouth but closed it and then left to do his bidding. Very wise decision, because if any bullshit comment came out of his mouth about Alana, he would lay him out on his fucking back. Brother or not.

Alana's eyes followed Chase's retreating form. "He doesn't understand why I'm here."

"Fuck him."

Her gaze bounced back to his. "Really?"

"Yep." He sat in front of her on the coffee table. "This is my house, so fuck him."

A dry laugh came from her. "I really am sorry. I just didn't know what to do. Seeing all my stuff destroyed like that?" She bit down on her lip and closed her eyes briefly. When they reopened, her stare fixed over his shoulder.

Chase returned with a glass of amber liquid. Chandler didn't give him the chance to hand it to her. Intercepting the glass, he waited until Alana lifted her hands. "Drink this," he ordered, somewhat surprised when she obeyed.

Alana took a huge gulp and immediately sputtered.

"Slowly." Chandler chuckled. "It's a bit strong."

"Yeah," she muttered, taking another tiny sip.

Chase lingered by them, his brows pinched. "Is everything okay?"

He opened his mouth, but Alana lifted her gaze. "Yes. Everything is fine. I'm just . . ." She took another sip, her stare once more fixing over Chandler's shoulder. "Chad's playing?"

Both men looked behind them, forgetting what they were watching. Chase folded his arms. "Yes. He's in Atlanta."

Her knuckles were bleached white from how tight she was holding the glass. "How is he? And Bridget?"

Chandler knew what she was doing. Redirecting the questions. He'd humor her. "They're doing great. Thanks to you."

His brother opened his mouth again, but Chandler cut him off with a warning glare. "How're the wedding plans going?" she asked, oblivious to the brothers' silent exchange.

Chase cleared his throat. "It's going."

"They plan to marry in June," Chandler said, giving a little more detail. He ignored the way his brother stiffened. Damn it, he was starting to get pissed. Yes, Alana hadn't gone easy on Chad and had blackmailed Bridget, but she wasn't a fucking terrorist hell-bent on destroying their lives. "I think they're planning to hold off on the honeymoon until after the season's over."

"That makes sense." She finished off the whiskey, staring

at the screen. "That's all . . . very nice. They make such a great couple."

Ten levels of awkward silence descended on the room, and anyone with an ounce of common sense would've bounced by now, but Chase looked like he was glued to his spot. Turning to his brother, Chandler pinned him with a look until Chase rolled his eyes.

"Okay. Well, I'm going to go get some ginger ale and crackers." Chase headed toward the dining room, stopping long enough to look back at Chandler. "I'll be calling."

Chandler ignored him, taking the glass from her hands. "How are you feeling? You were looking a little wobbly out there."

"I'm fine." She smiled, but it was painfully forced. "Ginger ale and crackers?"

"Maddie is sick." He caught himself, probably realizing she didn't know who he was talking about. "Madison Daniels. She's—"

"I know who she is. All of you were really close with her family, correct?"

He nodded slowly, leaning forward until his knees pressed into hers. "The Danielses are the only family my brothers and I really claimed. We spent most of our youth with them. In reality, they basically raised the three of us, plus Maddie and her brother."

"I was raised by my grandmother. My mom wasn't fit to raise me. She was . . . Well, she had issues." Her features pinched, as she appeared to realize the little piece of knowledge she'd shared. She lifted a hand to her hair, smoothing the tiny strands. He caught it on the way down, capturing her much smaller hand between his. She jerked back but couldn't pull free. "What are you doing?"

"Your hand is ice cold, Alana."

She wet her lips, and his eyes zeroed right in on that. Despite how obviously stressed she was, his cock swelled in response. He wanted to taste those lips with his tongue.

He wanted to taste a lot of her.

But that, unfortunately, was going to have to wait.

Lifting his gaze to hers, he held her stare as he picked up her other hand. Capturing them both, he slowly rubbed them between his, warming them up. "What kind of issues?"

Her dark eyes were unfocused behind the glasses. "What?"

One side of his lips tipped up. "Your mother. What kind of issues did she have?"

Color invaded her cheeks and a bit of sharpness returned to her gaze. "That's a personal question."

"You brought it up." He slid his hands up, his fingers reaching under the cuffs of her suit jacket. "Don't blame me."

She held his stare and several seconds passed. "She had a drinking problem. And a drug problem. And a boyfriend problem."

"That's a lot of problems," he murmured, admittedly surprised. For some reason, he'd pictured Alana coming from a two-parent household. Stiff. Logical. A bit boring, but a fully functional family nonetheless. "Our mother had a drinking and prescription pill problem. Father also had a girlfriend problem."

"That had to be tough. The girlfriend problem, considering he was married."

He smirked. "It was."

Alana's gaze finally flickered away, and her lashes lowered. For a moment, she sat there, letting him rub her hands. They were warm by now, but he couldn't make himself stop. Her skin was soft, her hands delicately formed. Didn't take any stretch of imagination to picture the rest of her body as beautifully formed.

"And that doesn't bother you?" she asked quietly.

Shrugging a shoulder, he spread his thighs a little, giving himself room. How he could still be hard talking about this shit was beyond him. "Did it suck for our mom and us as kids? Fuck yes, it did, but that's the way life is sometimes. It messed with Chase and Chad a little."

"But not you?"

"People get married when they shouldn't. They settle because they think they need to or it's what's expected from them. It happens every day, several times a day. Two people come together who shouldn't stay together. I'm smart enough to realize that there are cases where people meet and they should be together and just because my parents fucked up their lives, it doesn't mean I will or should." He paused but kept his hands moving over hers. "It is what it is."

A wry grin appeared, barely reaching her eyes. "That's what they say."

He slid closer, using his knee to slide between hers. The position was intimate, noted by her when her eyes flew back to his. She pulled her hands again and this time he let her go, but he didn't move away. He knew he was crowding her.

"I'm sorry." She started to rise. "I shouldn't be bothering you with this—any of this. You only agreed to look into the names I'd given you. I can go to a hotel until, well, this blows over. I should—"

"No," he said, his muscles tensing, prepared to tackle her if necessary.

She froze and her eyes widened behind her glasses. The haunted look was still there. "No?"

"Right now, it's not safe for you to go *back* to that hotel." He almost smiled when her eyes widened. "And this stalker also knows where you're staying and took it out on your apartment."

Folding her arms over her chest, she lifted her chin a fraction of an inch. "Then what am I supposed to do if I don't go to a hotel? I don't have anyone to go to. Okay? The only family I even claim is dead and I don't have any close friends here who I'd feel comfortable unloading this crap on. So what the hell exactly should I do? Sleep in my office or my rental car?"

"I'll take the job," he said.

"What?"

"I know you understood what I said. I'll take the job as your bodyguard. No one else at my company. Me. And you're not staying in a hotel any longer." As soon as the idea popped in his head, it felt *right*. It was what he wanted for various reasons. Some of them having nothing to do with the psycho out there, making her life a living hell, and while it may make him a grade-A bastard, he simply wanted her *here*.

Alana stared at him, her lips slightly parted.

"As entertaining as arguing with you is, this I'm not going to argue with you over. No to the hotel," he said again, tone firm. "You'll stay here."

Chapter Seven

What am I doing here?

Alana hadn't really remembered the drive to Chandler's house and she honestly didn't know why she'd searched him out. Well, that was a lie. For obvious reasons, she felt safe with him, and right now she needed to feel that.

Seeing her apartment and her belongings destroyed like that did more than rattle her. Fear, confusion, and anger over the lack of control swirled inside her, making her feel out of it, as if all of this was a horrible dream. But she shouldn't have come here, forcing her issues upon Chandler. He'd assumed the role of her bodyguard, but shouldn't there be a contract or something? This just seemed so inappropriate. In the recesses of her mind, she had to have known that when she got in the car and drove to his house.

What am I doing here?

That question kept playing over and over in her head, but it didn't change the fact that she was here, in a room that was as big as her master at home. Walls were painted in a deep olive, and the wood floors and dark headboard gave the room an earthy feel that was relaxing.

But she couldn't relax. God knew she was high-strung on any given day, but this was like a million times worse.

She'd been hiding upstairs for damn near close to an hour while Chandler was downstairs, most likely waiting for her, and she knew she needed to get her ass down there.

But she needed a few more minutes.

Sitting on the edge of the queen-size bed, she smoothed her fingers down her cheeks. Her hair slid forward, slipping over her shoulders and shielding her face. Her glasses sat forgotten on the nightstand.

Chandler had loaned her a pair of his old flannel pajama bottoms and a shirt that couldn't have fit his broad build since high school. It nearly swallowed her whole and it smelled of him—a mix of clean laundry and the faint trace of cologne she couldn't place.

With trembling hands, she lifted the hem of the borrowed shirt and inhaled the scent.

She was *sniffing* his shirt.

Good God, what was wrong with her? That was just so . . . so creepy and totally inexcusable.

Dropping the shirt, she wrapped her arms around her waist. Her skin was chilled to the bone and her insides felt ripped open, like what had been done to all her personal items. To do something so violent and pointless was beyond her. Who could seriously hate her this much? Tears welled up in her eyes, but she refused to let them fall. Even though she was alone, she didn't want to break like this. It was weak, a sign of no control.

Oh, but it stung like an angry wasp, to know someone hated her so. That someone would attempt to terrorize her, vandalize her car, stalk her, and then break into her apartment. A single tear snuck out, coursing down her cheek, reaching her fingertips.

What would've happened if she had been home? A shudder rocked her. She had no idea at what time the crime had been committed, the police didn't either, and she was late getting home from work tonight. There was a very real possibility that someone could've been waiting for her and when she hadn't shown, he'd taken his aggression out on her apartment. Another quake worked its way through her.

Where were her brass balls? She surely could use them now.

A throat clearing intruded on her thoughts, startling her. She jumped from the bed and spun around. Hastily, she wiped at any trace of tears.

Chandler stood in the doorway, his mouth open as if he were about to say something, but then either forgot or decided against it. His gaze, a startling, intense azure, traveled across her face as if it was the first time he'd laid eyes on her. His stare dropped to her lips, and she felt a flush crawl down her throat, following his gaze all the way to the tips of her toes. When his eyes made it back to hers, she sucked in a sharp breath.

She felt branded by his stare.

The tips of her breasts tingled and then hardened, pebbling against the satin and his borrowed shirt. A sensual thrill sent chill bumps across her skin. He looked at her like he wanted to devour her. She tried not to like the feeling that brought forth in her—the crazy rush of excitement and anticipation—but it pooled low in her belly nonetheless.

"You should wear your hair down more often," he said. Alana blinked slowly. "What?"

"Your hair," he repeated as he leaned against the doorframe, crossing his arms as he spread his legs. With his eyes all blue fire and the small grin full of lazy arrogance, he really was quite stunning. The picture of masculine beauty. "You're an attractive woman, but with your hair down and those glasses off, you really are quite beautiful."

As his words sank in, she snorted. She knew she didn't look like she face-planted an ugly branch, but beautiful? Yeah, that was not the case. If anything, Alana was exceptionally plain with her dark hair and eyes. "Beautiful? Removing my glasses and letting my hair down isn't a drastic makeover."

"If I say you're beautiful, then you're beautiful."

She arched a brow. "Oh, you're the deciding law on this?"

The lazy grin spread. "I am. So I don't want you wearing your hair in that bun anymore. Makes you look like you're ten times older than you obviously are."

"Are you fucking serious?"

"I am *fucking* serious." He cocked his head to the side. "I like the glasses, though. Reminds me of this teacher I had in high school. Every time they slipped down her nose, it made my—"

"Enough!" She held up her hands. "I totally get the picture, but you don't get to tell me how to wear my hair."

"I'm your bodyguard."

Staring at him, she gave a quick shake of her head. The man was insufferable—sexy, but incredibly insufferable. But within the matter of minutes, he'd yanked her out of

89

her self-pity and the tight grasp of fear, and for that she was thankful.

Didn't mean she had to accept any of what was coming out of his mouth or follow through with the crazy idea of her staying in his home. "You being my bodyguard doesn't mean you're my personal stylist, Chandler, and I can't—"

"Speaking of personal stylist, you look better in my old clothes than you do in those God-awful suits you wear. And trust me, you look fucking hot in my clothes."

Her cheeks tightened with a blush she wished would go away and die. "Thanks," she gritted out.

"Thank God the clothes in your closet were destroyed. See? There's a silver lining in every dark cloud or whatever bullshit they say. We can go shopping tomorrow and find you something that actually makes you look good."

Too pissed to be hurt by his comments, she curled her hands into fists at her sides. There was a good chance she was going to punch him in the face. "First off, fuck you."

His blue eyes gleamed with mischief. "I like where this is heading."

Correction: she *was* going to kick him in the balls. "Secondly, I'm so glad that my entire wardrobe being destroyed is such good news to you. Thirdly, I'd rather run in front of a speeding city bus than go clothes shopping with you."

"Well, that sounds drastic."

Her jaw ached from how hard she was clenching her teeth. "And finally, I can't stay here."

The laziness in his posture vanished in an instant and he straightened. "You're staying here, Alana."

"I can go back to the hotel—"

"Absolutely not," he interrupted, eyes flashing cobalt. "It is not safe for you to stay in a hotel."

A dull shard of dread hit her in the chest, but she ignored it. "I'm fine at the hotel."

"If you really believe that, then why did you come here?"

Ah, he had a good point. "That was a mistake, but there're tons of people around and—"

He unfolded his muscular arms. "Exactly. There are tons of people who go in and out all day and all night long. It's a major security threat, and I should've pulled your ass out of there the first night."

It still struck her speechless for a moment to know that he'd been watching her when she'd thought he'd forgotten about her. "I'm not staying here. It's absurd. It's your home, Chandler. It's so inappropriate."

One dark brow arched. "Who gives a fuck about appropriate?"

"I do!"

A look of impatience crossed his face. "You worry about what other people think too much."

"It's my job," she replied crossly.

"No." He shook his head and several shorter strands escaped the ponytail. "It's more than that. You job isn't your life—it shouldn't be."

"It's not yours?"

He laughed. "Hell no."

Her mouth opened, but she found she had no idea what to say. Better yet, how did they get so far off topic?

"Besides, your inappropriate argument is moot. I'm

your bodyguard. So if you stayed in that hotel, I'd be staying with you. But staying here is sure as hell a lot more comfortable."

Once again, he had a point, but she couldn't do this. Coming to CCG Security might have been the right thing to do, but she had been wrong in demanding that it be him. There had to be someone else, because she . . . she didn't trust herself around him. The way he made her feel, even now when she wanted nothing more than to karate chop him into next week, was the same feeling she saw in her mother's eyes every time she'd talked about a new guy.

"I'm fine with someone staying with me in a hotel room," she decided, lifting her chin stubbornly. "But it has to be someone else. Anyone but you, because—"

One second he was standing by the bedroom door and the next he was in front of her, one hand on her hip and the other delving deep into her hair, cradling the nape of her neck. The words formed on her tongue, but he silenced them with his lips.

Chandler kissed her.

Shock radiated down her spine. That had to be the only reason she didn't knee him between the thighs right off the bat. At first, it was barely a touch, but her lips tingled hotly, as if she'd dared to kiss the sun. His lips swept over hers once more as she placed her hands on his chest, prepared to push him away, but then he nipped at her lower lip. A tiny bite that brought forth a wave of tight lust that seemed to come out of nowhere. He nibbled at the corner of her lip as he pulled her against him, trapping her hands between them.

Good Lord, he kissed like a man starving for a taste.

Working at the tight seam of her lips, he pressed forward, demanding that she open up to him.

She couldn't help her reaction to the kiss, no matter how badly she wished she wasn't affected by it. She wanted to remain aloof to the sensual assault, to remain in complete control of herself, but a longing rose deep inside her, spreading like wildfire.

Her lips parted on a sigh, and Chandler delved inside, slowly probing the recesses of her mouth. He tasted of whiskey and something richer, deeper. The kiss deepened, and instead of pushing him away, her hands fisted in the shirt he wore, holding him in place. He kissed her like he could claim her with his tongue, and damn if he wasn't close to doing it.

As his mouth melted against hers, her hands spasmed around his shirt, and then it happened. She tentatively flicked her tongue against his, kissing him back. His answering growl rumbled through his chest and his grip on her tightened.

When he finally lifted his head, she was panting and her stare was unfocused. "You taste just as I imagined," he said huskily, loosening his hold on her and putting some space between them. "And I have a vivid imagination. You taste sweet."

"Why?" she demanded, placing her hand over her lips. She felt unsteady, as if she'd topple right over if he hadn't still been holding her by the nape of her neck.

One side of his lips tipped up. "I figured it was the only way to get you to stop arguing."

Alana stared up at him, stunned that he'd used that tactic. "You kissed me to shut me up?"

"Basically." The smug grin appeared as he tipped his chin down. Those shorter strands grazed his cheeks. "It worked, didn't it?"

She jerked away, breaking his hold and stumbling back a step. Anger infused her cheeks, chasing at the pleasant pleasure his lips had given her. Now she *was* offended. "You kissed me just to shut me up? You overbearing, inappropriate son of a—"

Chandler caught her once more and kissed her again. This time there was no sweet brush of his lips or barely there touch. He delved right in, soaking her up and kissing her until she couldn't breathe. A bone-deep wanting exploded, making her swollen and hot, but she cocked back her arm, punching him in the stomach.

A laugh burst from him as he caught her wrist and then her other, intercepting before she could get another indignant hit in. "Ouch, that could've hurt."

"I hope it did!" she seethed, torn between being turned on and ticked off. "You just can't go around kissing people to get them to stop talking."

"And why not?" He hauled her toward him as he took a step back. The next thing she knew, he was sitting on the edge of the bed and she was very much perched in his lap. "I thought it was actually really fun."

There had been times in Alana's life when she'd wondered how she got where she was. Her work? Determination. Gumption. Balls-to-the-walls type of approach. But this? She had no clue how she'd ended up sitting in Chandler's lap, her lips swollen from his kisses and her body burning for more while she seriously wanted to choke the ever-loving crap out of him.

Chandler looped his arms around her waist, the hold not tight but firm. She wasn't going anywhere, but she sure as hell wasn't going to sit here. She raised her hands, ready to do bodily harm.

"It wasn't the only reason I kissed you," he said.

Her eyes narrowed as her hands froze on his shoulders. "It's not?"

He dipped his chin, pressing his forehead to hers. His warm breath danced over her lips and her hands dropped to his shoulders, fingers digging into the tough muscle. "No, it's not. I've wanted to kiss you since you showed up at my door looking for Chad."

Surprise blasted through her like a bomb. He'd wanted to kiss her then? Alana knew she wasn't the kind of woman men typically lusted over for any length of time, but she believed him. She'd felt it in his kiss.

"And I'm serious," he continued, his lips grazing her cheek, eliciting a shiver from her. "You're not staying at a hotel. You're staying here." He drew back, so that his gaze locked with hers. "It's not going to be someone else. It'll be no one else but me."

Chapter Eight

Whoever came up with the idea to take this woman shopping was out of his fucking mind. Oh, yeah, that's right. It was *his* astonishingly dumb idea.

Alana was worse than a guy.

Chandler had to drag her into the shops, which she conveniently argued didn't carry the kind of clothing she'd wear. After about the fifth store, he refused to allow her to leave without purchasing enough clothes to get her through the week.

And then the arguing really began.

"That looks like a man's suit." He curled his lip in disgust at the black, drab suit she held in one hand.

Her eyes rolled. "It does not."

Poking at the blazer, he frowned. "Does it have shoulder pads? What year is this?"

Alana moved around a rack, muttering under her breath. He picked up words like "dick" and "asshole," among other sweet nicknames. "I guess you think I should be in skirts?"

He fought a smile as he cornered her between two more racks. "What's wrong with a skirt? I bet you have beautiful legs." He leaned in, and when her breath caught, he didn't mistake the sudden light in her dark eyes. Catching her gaze, he tipped his lips up as he reached around her and gently tugged on a loose strand of hair. It was soft as satin. "You wore your hair down today."

Her eyes flashed furiously behind her glasses. "Not because of you."

"Keep telling yourself that." As he straightened, he scanned the store for any oddballs. No one really looked out of place. The only man in the store was up at the counter, his back to them.

She tightened her fingers around a hanger until he thought she'd snap the plastic. By the looks of it now, he wouldn't believe that she'd actually sat in his lap last night for a few moments, calm and serene.

"The only reason I'm wearing my hair down is because someone came into my room while I slept, like a total freak, and took my bobby pins and hair bands."

Barely resisting the urge to laugh, he widened his eyes. "Really?"

She snorted, shoving that horrific suit back onto the rack. "You must have a small critter in your home that has an affinity for pins and rubber bands, because they were *also* missing from my purse."

He couldn't help it then. He laughed, and one would think they were knee-deep in a debate about politics or something actually relevant, based on how flushed her cheeks were. She shot him a glare that would have most men cupping themselves. It only made him hard as steel.

It took another thirty minutes to load her up with jeans,

linen pants, suits, and so on, and he finally saw the end in sight.

Guiding her back toward the dressing rooms, he kept an eye on their surroundings and a hand on her shoulder. Normally on his assignments, he made sure those who were under his protection were kept out of the public. He couldn't very well do that with her. She seriously had only the clothes he was lending her.

Hell, he really liked seeing her in his clothes. So this was a double dumb idea.

"Why are you scowling?" she demanded, the pile of clothes almost as tall as she was. "You're not the one being pushed around."

He leveled a mild stare at her as he pushed open an empty dressing room. "There you go."

"I do have two eyes in my head," she spat back, unceremoniously dumping her load on the floor. "Captain mother fucking obvious."

Raising a brow, he grinned. "Man, you really did wake up in a great mood this morning."

It was true. She had been as prickly as a hedgehog since she grumbled into his kitchen, her hair in cute disarray and her clothing rumpled. He should've been the one pissed off because he'd found her actually *cute,* like he was a girl or something, but she stole those rights right away from him. Instead of responding to his comment, she slammed the dressing room door in his face.

Chandler growled low in his throat, startling the woman sitting on the bench behind him.

"You don't scare me," came Alana's muffled voice

through the door. "Make all the animal noises you want. It's not me who comes across as needing a rabies shot."

"I beg to differ," he muttered, dropping onto another bench directly across from her room.

Today was the longest Saturday ever.

He'd already avoided two calls from Chad, which told him that the first thing Chase had done when Chad's game was over was call him and gossip like a woman. He'd have to talk to Chad at some point, but right now, there wasn't a pressing need for it. Hours had also passed since he'd spoken to Murray and asked him to check out Alana's apartment and gather as many personal items as he could. He hadn't heard back from him yet, so he wondered if Murray got himself arrested sneaking into Alana's apartment.

He was also tired, hungry, and horny. So fucking horny it was like being sixteen again. He went to bed hard, woke up hard, and was now sitting outside a dressing room, hard.

It had been a long time, if ever, since he'd wanted a woman this badly.

Tipping his head back against the partition wall, he scanned those shopping in the store. Last night, he'd barely gotten any sleep knowing that Alana was across the hall, and now he was paying for it. Half of it was his fault. He'd put the moves on her yesterday, kissing her. At first, she had frozen against it, but when she'd gotten into it, damn if she hadn't responded. Just thinking about Alana sliding her tongue against his had him bursting at the seams. He wanted to bust into the dressing room, take her home, and get her on her knees. Maybe even tie her wrists, spread her legs . . .

"What the hell?"

Chandler's head jerked up in time to see a scrap of red lace fly over the dressing room door. His lips split into a grin. When Alana had been busy arguing over the jeans he'd picked out, he'd slipped the teddy into her pile of clothing.

A second later, the door cracked open, revealing Alana's glare and pink cheeks. Her shoulders were bare with the exception of two tiny ivory straps. "You *pig*! I'm not sleeping in something that a stripper would wear when she's working the pole."

Now he was picturing Alana in the teddy working a pole. With her glasses on.

Her eyes narrowed dangerously, as if she knew the direction of his thoughts.

"That's okay." He stretched out his legs, crossing his ankles. He'd been wrong before. The end was nowhere in sight. "You can just sleep naked. I honestly like that idea better."

It was in the evening when Murray swung by, and Chandler's temper had been stretched thin. The whiskey he was nursing wasn't doing much to help.

"About damn time," he muttered.

Murray huffed. "That's not how you should answer the door."

Not in the mood to bullshit, he cut the crap. "Find anything?"

Edging past him, Murray carried in two large tote bags. "I brought whatever personal girlie stuff I could find. It took a while. The place was a complete mess."

"So it's as bad as we thought it was?" He led Murray into the kitchen, the farthest away from the stairs. He hoped Alana didn't come down, because rehashing the condition of her apartment surely wouldn't put her in a better mood.

Murray deposited the totes on the counter. "Absolutely fucking destroyed. Took a knife to anything that could be torn apart, even the walls. The fucker even emptied out her fridge. That's some major kind of rage."

Chandler rubbed an ache along his shoulder. The old wound gave him trouble from time to time. "Did he get inside the way I thought?"

He nodded. "Right through the sliding glass door. The woman needs an alarm system and needs to replace that door. Those are the worst possible pieces of shit ever."

"Find out anything else?" He picked up his glass of whiskey.

"Spoke to William Manafee. The man didn't have anything really nice to say about Miss Gore."

A flash of unexpected anger zinged through him. "What did he say?"

"Other than Miss Gore being a bitch of the highest order and that she destroyed his marriage?" Murray crossed the kitchen. "Nothing else. But I don't think it was him. Even though he's not a fan of the little publicist, there was a level of reluctant respect in his voice."

That did little to soothe his rising anger. From personal experience, he knew Alana was hard to deal with, but she *helped* these people, even his brother, and at great cost to herself. Was he the only person who seemed to understand that?

"I also went ahead and tried Van Gunten's agent," Murray continued. "She said that Jennifer wouldn't be available to speak with me until two weeks from now. She's on a movie set in Australia or some shit. Wasn't able to search down any of her friends, except the Ryan fella. It's definitely not him."

"How so?"

"Because he overdosed about three months ago." Helping himself, Murray grabbed a beer out of the fridge and propped a hip against the counter. "Did she mention anything about a message?"

Chandler's brows lowered. "No. What message?"

Popping the lid off the bottle, he took a quick swig before he answered. "In her home office, the words 'You lying whore' were carved into the wall."

Chandler's hand tightened around the glass. "No. She did not mention that."

"Maybe she didn't see it."

Anger whipped through his insides with acid-tipped barbs. "Seems like a hard thing to overlook."

Murray eyed him closely. "All depends on if she went into her home office and how shocked she was by seeing her apartment. I'm telling you, man. That placed was fucked up. She might not have noticed it." He took another gulp of beer and then tossed the bottle into the garbage. "Are you sure she's being honest with you?"

"About what exactly?" He finished off his glass of whiskey, reached for the bottle, and then thought better. Getting drunk off his ass wasn't the brightest idea.

"Are you sure there isn't an ex involved in this? I know

she told you there isn't, but the amount of damage was substantial. And calling her a lying whore? It all seems very personal."

He wished Murray would stop saying "lying whore," because it made him want to punch someone in the throat. And since Murray was the only person in front of him, he was the only target, and that sucked. He liked the guy.

"I know she apparently pisses people off on a daily basis, but this is personal," Murray added.

"She doesn't piss people off daily." The back of his neck burned. "She *helps* people."

Murray opened his mouth and then his eyes narrowed. Several seconds passed. "Where's she staying?"

"Here."

Silence. It stretched so long Chandler wondered if the man had lost the ability to speak, but finally Murray spoke. "Are you fucking serious?"

The burn on the back of his neck increased. "Are you?"

"She's staying here?" Murray's voice dropped low. "In your home?"

"Unless there's a different meaning for 'here' that I'm unaware of, then yes."

Murray stared at him like he'd whipped out his cock and started swinging it around. "Why not a hotel or somewhere less personal? Like we'd normally do in this situation? Or, I don't know, have her go to family and we run detail outside?"

"She doesn't have anyone else," he said, acting on the urge to defend what he was doing and her. But the moment those words left his mouth, he regretted them.

"Does she have you?" Murray shot back.

Chandler's eyes narrowed dangerously, but his voice remained level. "That's really none of your business."

Murray opened his mouth.

"I mean it, bud. Don't fucking push me on this. She's staying here with me and that's as far as I'm discussing it."

Holding up his hands, Murray shook his head. "Whatever. If you think this is a bright idea, then go with it. Not going to judge."

Chandler didn't respond and he didn't relax at those words.

"Where is she anyway? Hiding from you?"

His lips twitched at that. "Maybe."

"Wouldn't blame her for that." Murray headed for the door. "I'll let you know if I find out anything else on the celeb and friends."

"Okay." He started to close the door but stopped. "Oh, and can you—"

"Call and get someone out there to clean up her place?" Murray smiled broadly, and for some reason, it made the guy look scarier. "Already did it. Also got a security system ordered for her."

Muscles in his back eased a little. "You're awesome."

"I know."

After Murray left, Chandler made sure his place was locked down, alarm set, and then grabbed the totes before heading upstairs. What Murray had said about an ex nagged at him. Had he been incorrect and Alana had held back important information?

Whatever it might be, he was about to find out.

He started to knock on her bedroom door but found it

slightly cracked. Easing it open, he slipped into her room. Maybe he should've knocked, but what the hell? It was *his* house.

His gaze fell to the bed first, and it was empty. Shopping bags were stacked on the floor against the dresser. The room smelled of her—lilac and vanilla. His eyes moved to the door to the bathroom. It was also ajar and soft light edged around the bottom. Sitting the totes on the dresser, he was about to force himself out of the bedroom when a startled cry edged with terror erupted from the bathroom.

What the hell? What kind of trouble could she get herself into alone in a bathroom?

More than a little concerned, he moved toward the bathroom door. In the back of his head, he knew he should announce himself, but he pushed open the door.

And came to a complete stop, something tugging at his chest and causing the muscles to tighten in his stomach. Pulsing adrenaline coursed through him, and he couldn't remember why he even came up the stairs to find her before he'd heard her cry out.

Never in his life had he met a more contrary woman, but right then, she was the embodiment of wet dreams. Go figure it was when she might be asleep.

She must've had a nightmare that had passed over her. Now she rested peacefully, but a storm was raging inside his body.

Alana was in the tub, her head resting on a rolled-up towel, facing the door. A practically serene look marked her expression. He'd never really seen her as such. The tug in his chest was stronger this time, drawing him closer.

Her hair was piled up around her head, but without anything to hold it there, several tendrils hung down, drifting over her shoulders and into the water. The scent of shower gel filled the bathroom, which explained the frothy white bubbles that obscured her body except for the sweet swell of her chest and a gracefully bent knee.

Seeing her like this was a punch to the gut and caused his already hard cock to pulse against the zipper of his jeans.

Goddamn, it was the sexiest thing he'd ever seen. And he'd seen a lot of sexy in his life, but this—fuck yeah—this was stunning. Maybe it was the white-capped bubbles drifting over her skin or the way her plump lips were slightly parted. It could be the innocence of it all. How she slumbered without knowing he was there, watching her.

Or maybe it was just because it was *her*.

Alana shifted slightly. She let out a soft, contented sigh that boiled his blood. Her knee slipped under the water, stirring the bubbles. The peaks of her breasts broke the surface. Nipples dusty pink and tightened into little nubs, they were absolutely perfect.

Holy hell, he was . . . he was absolutely undone by the mere sight of them.

He must've made a sound or she finally sensed his presence, because her eyes suddenly flew open. She sucked in a startled breath.

Their eyes locked.

Alana jerked up, tucking her legs under her. Bubbles sloshed over the sides of the tub as she rose. Water sluiced down her body in thick rivulets, drawing his heated gaze.

For the best seconds of his life, she froze before him,

completely and splendidly naked. Her arms to her sides, tiny bubbles gliding down her skin, and all that beautiful flesh on display for him to devour. And boy, did he ever eat her up with his stare.

My God.

His mouth went dry as his balls tightened. As he suspected, she had been hiding a lush body under the shapeless suits. True, her breasts were small, but they were perfect for her narrow waist. Her hips flared out, sweetly rounded, and her thighs were shapely. In a second, he could picture them wrapping around his hips. She was bare between the thighs, with the exception of a neatly trim thatch of dark curls.

His once dry mouth watered. He wanted—no, *needed*—to touch her, to taste her. Every glorious inch of her. He *needed* to be on her, inside her. Especially between her thighs. He wanted to dive in with his tongue and then his cock.

Surprisingly, there was a small tattoo beside her hip to the right of her navel. It was a red rose, slight bent at the top. Three petals lay at the base of the green stem. Something about the design was familiar to him.

He dragged his eyes up, and there was no mistaking the lust in her gaze. The flush racing across her cheeks and down her throat told him that she saw his hunger. Her nipples tightened even more, and he groaned.

"You're the most fucking magnificent thing I've ever seen," he ground out.

Then those wonderful seconds came to an end. She reached over, snatched up a towel, and hastily wrapped it around her body. Her mouth opened and he knew she was about to give him an ass-chewing for the ages, but he wasn't going to let that happen. Not yet.

Chandler was on her before she took her next breath.

Chapter Nine

Holy fuck a duck . . .

Anger and embarrassment had flooded Alana's system, but so had something a hell of a lot more intense. Rife, intoxicating lust seized her—the same wild, out-of-control feelings that had taken her over the night before, when he'd kissed her. Knowing how quickly she'd lost herself in a simple kiss had dumped her in a bad mood all day. There was no reason for her to have such a strong reaction to a damn kiss and she shouldn't be that attracted to him.

But she was.

Now those feelings were back, stronger than before. Her breasts ached, her legs felt like jelly, and she was incredibly damp between her legs.

Alana knew she should have been pissed at Chandler and she was, but the hunger she felt inside her had been reflected in his brilliant blue gaze. And that yearning was more powerful than anything else she was experiencing.

Her fingers had tightened around the hasty knot she'd made in the towel above her breasts. She couldn't breathe. He'd been staring at her like she was the only woman in the world and he'd shuddered.

When he'd moved toward her, fast and graceful as any predator stalking its prey, there was no place for her to go. She wasn't even sure she wanted to run. No man had ever looked at her like he had.

It made her feel brazen and wanton and she *liked* it.

There was a brief moment when she'd wondered if this was how her mom had felt, if this was the first symptom to the slippery slope that was obsession. Then Chandler's large hands landed on her bare, damp shoulders at the same moment his lips met hers.

The kiss wasn't about a slow seduction or exploration. His mouth fused to hers and when she drew in a breath, he delved in. She felt his body tremble against her and she was amazed that he was the one who was shaking with need— need for *her*. That awed her, and as a hand swept to the back of her neck, she was carried away in the exquisite sensations he was opening in her.

Alana needed to tell him to stop. This wasn't appropriate. A relationship of any sort between them would never work. She placed her hands on his chest, but instead of pushing him away, she gripped the soft material, holding him to her.

She kissed him back, just as fiercely and with the same need that he claimed her mouth with. Her breasts tightened and swelled, aching with the want of his touch.

He groaned against her lips, causing a chill to skate over her flushed skin. "You have no idea what you do to me."

She had a feeling she could say the same about him, but then he kissed her again, and she wasn't thinking anymore. All she was focused on were the sensations he was dragging out in her, and there was something beautifully freeing in that. She fell headfirst into it, praying that when he was done with her, she would be able to resurface.

His hand slid down her bare arm and then dropped to her cloth-covered hip. He guided her head back and his lips left hers. A disappointed whimper escaped her lips, and Chandler chuckled deeply.

"I'm not done with you. Nowhere near it," he said, nipping at her chin. "I've only just gotten started."

Her stomach fluttered like a thousand butterflies had taken flight. "Really?"

"Oh yeah." He grinned and tilted her head to the side. He nibbled a path along her jaw to her ear, catching the lobe between his teeth. She gasped. "You like that, don't you?"

She couldn't answer. Her senses were spinning.

Chandler chuckled again as he dipped his head lower, blazing a line of hot, wet kisses down her neck. When he reached her pulse, his tongue flicked over her skin. She shifted restlessly, wanting more, knowing there was more.

His lips moved along the edge of the towel as his one hand moved up, resting at her rib cage, so close to her breasts. He didn't touch her there. No, he teased her with the lines of kisses, with the way his thumb moved in a circle over the towel, coming close to the swell but never quite touching her.

"Tell me you want this," he all but growled. Lifting her head, he kissed the corner of her parted lips. "Tell me you need this as badly as I do and you will not regret a second of this."

But wouldn't she? When it was all over and the heat of lust faded, how would she feel? There was already a part of her that was drawn to him, beyond the physical attraction. Would things be like they were before? Could she separate an act of lust from meaning anything else? Her mother had never been able to do that, so how could she be any different?

Chandler kissed her again, and panic clawed at her chest. From everything she knew about him, he wasn't the type of man to settle down, and from what she knew about his needs, she wasn't sure she could ever fulfill them. And she was also sure that every moment she allowed this to continue, the further she slipped under Chandler's sensual control. But she wasn't the type to settle down, either. And she was no coward.

She wanted to feel this—whatever this was. As long as she kept her head on straight and above water, she could handle him and her own conflicting feelings. Couldn't she? The flutter moved from her stomach to her chest. Maybe she wasn't even thinking straight, but who could blame her? This man was walking, breathing sin.

"Alana," he murmured, brushing his lips over hers. His breath was enticingly hot. "Tell me."

Blinking her eyes open, she barely contained a sigh when her eyes met his. "You are really impatient."

He grinned, and her chest spasmed at the almost boyish quality to it. "You have no idea."

Her hands smoothed out against his chest and trembled. He didn't look away, holding her stare with a level of passion that stirred tendrils of yearning deep inside her. "Should we be doing this?" she whispered.

"This is the only thing we should ever be doing." He

pressed his forehead against hers and slid his hand through her damp hair, twisting his fingers into the mass. He captured her in his hold. "I can promise you that there won't be a second of this you won't enjoy."

She wet her lips nervously and his gaze heated. "What about afterward?"

"What about it?"

Good question, but a dull ache pierced her chest. She pushed it away. "I don't just sleep around."

"I wasn't planning on doing any sleeping."

Her fingers curled as his words sent a spasm through her. "I don't have sex with just anyone."

Chandler made a deep sound in his chest. "I'm happy to hear that." He shifted slightly, drawing her closer to the edge of the tub. "You want this just as badly as I do."

God's honest truth, she did. Her body trembled with the thought of it, but it had been so long since she'd been with anyone that she doubted her vagina would even know what to do. "I do, but . . ."

His tongue flicked over her lips with a dark promise as the hand under her breasts slid around the small of her back. "How about this. No sex."

"No sex?"

He laughed. "Let me clarify. No penetration. We'll take this slow."

Alana understood what he was saying, but her brain was slow to process it. He didn't want to have sex with her? At least not full-out sex? There was a tiny part of her that was stupidly disappointed, but she refused to give much thought to that.

The hand on her back slipped lower, and she bit down on her lip to stop the moan building in her throat from escaping. What did she have to lose by taking what he was offering? They weren't going to actually have sex and she was a grown adult, more than capable of having a little fun.

As their eyes met, Alana was struck again by the hunger in his gaze. He wanted this—wanted her—and there was something unequivocally powerful in that. Before she could change her mind or let common sense intrude and leave her aching all night without fulfillment and in an even worse mood tomorrow, she nodded.

Chandler froze, his mouth inches from hers. "Is that a yes?"

She nodded again.

"Say it," he said in a low, almost dangerous voice. "Say you want me to please you."

"Yes." Her voice was barely above a whisper and she was unable to look away from those dark-lashed eyes of his. "I want you to please me."

Chandler didn't hesitate.

Those words seemed to unlock something primal in him. He snaked an arm around her waist and lifted her from the tub. His strength shocked her, though she shouldn't have been surprised. While she'd hid—i.e. sulked—upstairs after returning from their shopping trip, she'd seen him disappear into a room downstairs full of weights and exercise equipment. The man was all muscle.

Her feet didn't touch the floor until they were beside the bed. With a barely contained urgency, he stripped away the towel, and cool air rushed over her flushed skin. She moved to cover herself, but he caught her arms.

"Don't hide from me." His gaze traveled over the length of her body, lingering in some areas longer than other. "You're beautiful."

She let out a nervous laugh. "I'm already naked. You don't have to ply me with compliments."

"I mean it." He took her hand as he sat on the bed. Lifting his head, he stared up at her. Staying before him completely naked while he was clothed had her at a disadvantage. He tugged her between his thighs and then settled his hands on her hips. "I want to look my fill, so when it's later and I'm alone, all I have to do is close my eyes to see your body while I make myself come."

Holy God, her ears were scorched.

"Do you do that a lot?" she asked, breathless.

"Jerk off?" His lips tipped up as he moved his large hands along the curve of her waist, stopping below her aching breasts. His searching gaze seared her body. "Or jerk off thinking about you? The answer is yes to both."

Her breath stilled in her chest as he felt the light weight of her breasts, his fingers coming tantalizingly close to their peaks. "You're lying."

"I never lie." The conviction in his voice was undeniable. "Every single fucking night since you showed up at my door. I'd send you running if I told you what some of my fantasies involved."

She wanted to know. Details—lots of details, but then his fingers moved over her breasts and the ability to speak went out the window. Catching her nipples between his fingers, he watched her closely as he rolled them with his thumb and then plucked at them. They hardened and ached for him.

"You were having a nightmare," he said quietly, teasing her.

"W-what?"

"When you were bathing. I heard you cry out," he explained. "That's why I came in there."

"Oh." Her thoughts were muddled in a sensual haze. "It was just a dream."

He pulled her closer and then his mouth was on her breast, licking over the peak and then tugging on it with his teeth. The sharp burst of pleasured pain was instantly soothed with a lap of his tongue. He alternated between the quick nips and licks until her head fell back. She cried out, her body shuddering even as it tightened deliciously.

Chandler suddenly pulled back, and her eyes flew open. She stared at him in disbelief. "You stopped!"

"For now." He sent her a fleeting grin and then pulled his shirt off over his head.

His body . . . she hadn't forgotten how perfect it was. The broad, muscled shoulders, hard pecs, and a stomach that was rippled and chiseled like rock. He was 100 percent male, not an inch of flab on his body. Her gaze found a puckered, circular scar on his shoulder, the skin a deeper pink than the rest of his body. She wanted to ask how he got it, because to her, it really looked like a bullet wound.

"Turn around."

Her brows shot up. "What?"

Holding his shirt between his hands, he spun it until it was stretched long and thin. His eyes met hers and a dark, dangerous allure filled the blue of his eyes. "Turn around, Alana."

Her heart jumped in her chest as a sharp, almost painful lick of pleasure pulsed through her. Her eyes fixed on his shirt, and she couldn't help but think about what he wanted to do with it and all the things she'd heard about how Chandler liked to give pleasure. Part of her wanted to be turned off by it, to be disgusted, but she wasn't.

Every cell in her body swelled. A tiny spark of fear blossomed in her chest, but it wasn't that she was afraid of him. More like afraid of how she'd respond. But she took a deep breath and did as he asked.

A hand grazed over the curve of her bottom, causing her to jerk. She felt him behind her, standing. The heat from his body warmed hers. "Chandler?"

"Do you trust me?" he asked, skimming a hand over her hip and then to her arm. He pulled it back behind her. "You have to trust me for this. Do you?"

Her heart pounded in her chest as she swallowed. "Yes."

"That's my girl." He pressed a kiss to her shoulder and then guided her other arm back behind her.

She knew what he was going to do, but it still came as a shock when she felt the cloth draping over her wrists. A dark thrill that should've surprised her lit up her blood and scattered her senses. Was he . . . ?

Chandler tightened the makeshift bond, securing her wrists behind her back. So the rumors and the whispered talk about Chandler were dead-on.

He turned her around, but she kept her gaze trained on the line between his pecs. "Hey," he said, placing the tips of his fingers under her chin and guiding her gaze up. "You have to be okay with this. If not—"

"I'm okay." She wiggled her fingers and tested the bonds. She could move her hands, but not far. Heat coursed over her cheeks. "I'm just . . ."

"Fucking stunning?" he supplied, and her lips cracked into a grin. He clasped her cheeks and lowered his mouth to hers.

The kiss was different. Slower. Deeper. He tasted her, drawing her deep within him, and she melted into the touch. With a deep, animalistic groan, he shifted, and the next second she was on her back and he hovered above her. The look in his eyes caused the air to catch in her throat.

"Look at you." He slid a palm between her breasts, stopping below her navel. "I could stare at you forever."

"I hope not."

"Patience," he murmured, lowering his head.

Patience was not a virtue she appreciated, but Chandler wasn't going to be sped up. He took his time kissing her lips, and then he ran his mouth along her jaw, down her throat, and between her breasts. He tongued the soft swell of her breast, traveling up and then around the aching point. He came so close, but always skated away at the last second. Her nipples were pouty, hard, and aching by the time his hot mouth covered one.

Her back arched clear off the bed as he suckled deep and nipped, going back and forth between her breasts until her head was spinning.

Just when she was about to beg him to stop, for more, he kissed a path down to her navel. His tongue flicked inside and she felt an answering jolt between her thighs.

"Why this?" he asked, tracing the tattoo with his wicked tongue.

Her hands curled helplessly behind her as she closed her eyes. "Because ..."

"Because why?"

She didn't want to answer, because it was rather embarrassing.

Chandler chuckled. "You'll tell me eventually."

"No, I won't."

"Is that a challenge?" He kissed each of the three withered petals.

A smile tugged at her lips as the gesture also pulled at her heart. The kisses ... They were tender. "Isn't there something else you could be doing with your mouth besides talking?"

"Oh, listen to you." Chandler's lips left her stomach and she opened her eyes in time to see him crawl up her. His eyes were like blue pools. "I have a thing for that mouth." He dipped his head, kissing her deeply. "That I plan to put to use very soon."

She drew in a bated breath and the tips of her breasts brushed his chest. The sparse, wiry hairs teased her. "Are you sure? I might fall asleep before then."

Chandler laughed, dropping his head to nuzzle her neck. He made his way back down her body, nipping and licking until his head was poised between her thighs. Her breathing was coming fast and ragged by then. Men had gone down on her before, and she'd never been a big fan of it, but she knew with Chandler it was going to be different. Sex before had never been like this.

He peered up at her as he rested on his side, one arm hooked under a thigh and his shoulders splitting her legs. He ran a finger around the patch of hair. "Tell me about the tattoo."

"No."

His finger moved lower and she tensed. "When did you get it done?"

She closed her eyes and clamped her lips together, wishing she could just grab his head and put his mouth to better use. *"Chandler."*

"Tell me when." His finger traveled up the inside of her thigh, stopping just below her heat. "How old were you?"

The bastard was relentless. Her skin burned and her body pulsed with yearning. "I was eighteen," she bit out.

"Happy?"

"Yes." He cupped her between the thighs, covering her throbbing center. "Happy?"

Her back bowed as her hips immediately pushed against his hand. "Getting there . . ."

"Hmm." He pressed a kiss to the crease of her thigh as he rotated his palm, eliciting a throaty moan from her. "Drunk or sober?"

"What?" she gasped.

He pressed his palm against her. "Were you drunk or sober when you got the tattoo?"

She wanted to refuse him, but then he lifted his hand. Cool air brushed her and she muttered a curse. Chandler laughed. "I was a little drunk," she admitted, and was rewarded with a long finger trailing down her swollen folds. "Oh God . . ."

"A little drunk? Like you're a little wet right now?"

Her cheeks flushed. "Something like that."

"The rose looks familiar to me," he said casually, just as he slipped his finger inside her tightness. "What is it from?"

Alana arched, sucking in a deep breath. He slowly moved his finger in and out as he pressed against the bundle of nerves. Her whole body trembled and her breasts strained upward.

He added another finger, stretching her. "Damn, you're so tight."

Every part of her felt incredibly taut, as if she were seconds from bursting. Her stomach quivered and fine darts of pleasure zinged through her. Her release coiled deep inside her, drawing her body into one fine point.

Then he stopped, withdrawing those wonderful fingers. "Alana?"

Her eyes opened into slits. He stared back at her, mischief in his smile but a dark hunger in his eyes. He would drag this on until she went crazy and he'd love every second of it. But she couldn't take the sublime aching any longer.

"It's the rose from *Beauty and the Beast*," she admitted.

"What?"

"You know? The rose that wilts and is enchanted?" She let her head fall back and closed her eyes. "It was my favorite movie as a kid and I was drunk one night. Ended up with the tattoo."

Silence stretched out to the point that she feared he'd grown bored with this game, but the next second she felt his warm breath moving over her and her entire body tensed.

Then he kissed her where she ached so badly.

A strangled cry left her lips, heightened with one sinfully deep swipe of his tongue. Intense pleasure bloomed as he continued to lick her, slipping deep inside and then coming out, circling the sensitive nub above. Then he slid a finger into her and he clasped down on her clit, matching the thrusts of his fingers to his mouth.

Never had Alana felt something so intense as this. Pressure clamped down on her, dragging her under. She desperately fought her response, but her hips twitched and then she was thrusting against his skilled hand and mouth shamelessly, her head moving to and fro as her breath quickened in her chest.

"Let go," he urged hotly. "Just let go and let me please you. Let go."

Each pull of his mouth caused her to cry out. With her hands bound, she couldn't grasp onto anything, couldn't center herself in the midst of the sharp waves of pleasure. She was absolutely helpless to him and to the desires ravaging her body. He inserted another finger and his teeth scraped her sensitive flesh and then she did let go.

Alana exploded. The tension unraveled so quickly inside her that she screamed out his name as spasms racked her body. She shattered and flew apart, shaken to the core as her release showered sparks through her. He rode her out through it all, wringing every rolling crest of pleasure from her.

Only when she'd sunk back into the mattress, boneless and breathless, did he stop. Pressing a kiss to her inner thigh and then below her navel, he rose up, taking her mouth. The taste of him and her was like being intoxicated.

God, she hoped she didn't end up with a tattoo of a singing teacup by the end of the night.

Chandler smoothed his palm up her side, cupping her breast. "Beautiful," he said, rubbing the tip of his nose over hers. "You're absolutely beautiful when you lose control."

After an orgasm, Alana was like a contented kitten instead of the tigress ready to rip into him with her sharp claws. She relaxed against him for a few moments while he regained control of himself.

He was about to lose it without taking his jeans off.

Never had he been so fucking turned on while giving a woman pleasure. He was so aroused that it was actually painful, but he forced himself to lay beside her, idly brushing his thumb over the rosy pink peak of her breast. He liked her nipples and her breasts and the way she tasted like honey on his lips and how she plumped her lips and . . .

Hell, he just *liked* her.

But "like" was a weak word to describe the way his heart was pounding in his chest like a jackhammer. Leaning over her, he kissed the tip of her breast. He smiled when she shuddered and then sighed. Lifting his stare, he let his gaze travel over her face. It had to be one of the rarest moments when she looked absolutely relaxed, lips parted and eyes closed. Thick, dark lashes fanned her cheeks.

He wasn't waxing poetic bullshit, earlier. To him, she was absolutely beautiful.

Her lashes fluttered open. "That was . . ."

"Amazing?" He arched a brow. "I know."

A soft, tinkling laugh came from her, and there was a

spasm somewhere near his chest. "Your modesty is amazing."

He smiled.

She struggled to rise as her arms were still tied behind her back. He started to set her free, but her words stopped him. "What about you?"

Both brows rose. "What about me?"

Her gaze dropped to where a bulge strained against his pants and she wet her lips. His cock jerked in response. "You said earlier that you planned on putting my mouth to good use."

He had said that, and fuck if he didn't want that more than anything he'd ever wanted in his life, but he . . .

Chandler shook his head.

Her tongue moved against her lips and whatever tiny level of hesitation that had been brewing in his chest evaporated like smoke. Her eyes were wide and dark with passion, hair a tumbled mess over her shoulders and curling around her breasts. It was the first time he'd seen her look so . . . so *free*.

And fuck, she was perfect.

"Well then . . ." He rose, unbuttoning his pants. He had them off in less than a second.

Her gaze dropped, and she made a sound that his cock really liked. He was hard, jutting up in the air, and so close to losing it that if she kept staring at him like that, he'd come right then.

Gripping her shoulders, he positioned her on her knees before him and then bent down, capturing her lips in a searing kiss that ended too soon. Then he straightened before her.

With her wrists secured behind her back, her chest thrust up and her eyes wide, he could absolutely eat her up, one lick at a time. And he was sorely tempted to do that again, but she tipped up her chin, meeting his gaze.

"What is it that you wanted me to do?" Her voice was breathy.

Like he thought before, she was fucking perfect.

He wrapped his hand around the base of his cock, moisture already beaded on the head. "Suck me."

Something downright wicked flared in her eyes, and then she ducked her chin. Her hair slid forward, obscuring her face. He felt her breath first and his balls tightened, and then her hot, wet mouth slipped over the head of his cock.

His back bowed as he groaned. She took him, sliding her tongue along the head as she shifted on the bed, balancing herself on her knees. He gathered her hair with his free hand and tilted her head so she could take him deeper, and she did.

Alana nearly swallowed his length and that was no easy feat.

She moved her head up and down, swirling her tongue as she sucked long and hard. Every muscle in his body tightened. He tried to hold still, but when her teeth grazed his sensitive head, he couldn't hold back.

His hips thrust forward as he watched her cheeks sink in as she tugged on his cock. Her lashes swept up and their gazes collided for an instant. Something in her stare broke him wide open. Release powered down his spine. He tried not to pull back, but she followed him and if he hadn't stopped, she would've fallen right off the bed. The fucking sight of her obliterated his senses. The way her body curved toward his, how she was so willing with her hands tied behind her back.

It was too much.

He came, his hips jerking wildly, and she kept on him, humming soft sounds of pleasure. He emptied into her hot mouth, shouting hoarsely as he spasmed endlessly. The orgasm . . . *Goddamn* . . . it felt like it would never end. His hand tightened against the back of her head, holding her until the last achingly perfect pulse.

Slowly, he eased away from her, his legs strangely weak as he dragged in a deep breath. He dropped his gaze to hers, his chest rising and falling raggedly. "Are you okay?"

Alana nodded as she bit down on her lip. "Are you?"

He coughed out a laugh. "Fucking perfect."

Pink stained her cheeks as she averted her gaze. She sat back on her legs, letting out a little yawn. She was exhausted and he should let her be. Both of them had sought and found their pleasure, but he wasn't ready.

After experiencing her mouth on him and the taste of her, there was no way this was going to be the last time. Quickly untying her wrists, he all but toppled onto his back, pulling her naked body to his, and draped a possessive arm over her waist, fitting her close. She was stiff against him, her back too straight and her arms awkwardly stuck between their damp bodies. So cuddling wasn't her thing?

He wasn't a big fan of it, either, but strangely, he wanted her beside him, and she was going to have to deal with it.

When he had her where he wanted, he gathered her wrists in his hands and began to massage the skin.

Slowly, as the seconds turned into minutes, Alana relaxed against him. Her breath evened out, and her body melted into his.

There was no way in hell Chandler was letting her go anytime soon.

Chapter Ten

Chandler ended up falling asleep Saturday night in her room, sprawled gloriously naked across her bed and with his arm possessively thrown over her waist. Admittedly, she had never been more comfortable in her life pressed up against him, with no barrier separating their flesh, but she couldn't allow herself to sleep while he snored softly.

Lovers slept together after sex, not two people who were getting off.

In her past, albeit brief, relationships, she'd had trouble sleeping in the same bed. Even with Steven, who had been the longest relationship she'd been in, she'd never been able to relax enough to comfortably sleep. And that had to mean something, right?

But last night . . . Oh God, after about an hour, her lids had grown too heavy to keep open and she had relaxed into him. The realization had jerked her awake and in a near panic, she had slipped free from his grasp, gathered up her clothes, and slept on the couch downstairs.

She'd spent the vast majority of Sunday morning and after avoiding Chandler, who seemed okay with it. The few times they'd crossed paths in the house hadn't been pleasant for either of them. He seemed mad at her, but for what, she wasn't sure.

Part of her didn't regret what had transpired between them Saturday night. Good Lord, no. What he'd done to her would fuel her fantasies for a long time to come, but how was she ever to look at him again without feeling his hot mouth on her? How was she ever to forget?

Maybe she was overthinking things.

She was folding and refolding her newly acquired stash of clothing for the hundredth time when Chandler appeared in the doorway. The moment her gaze connected with his, heat zinged across her cheeks and she felt silly for blushing so easily.

"Hungry?" he asked, expression impassive.

Her stomach rumbled in response. All she had eaten earlier was a bagel with cream cheese. "What do you have in mind?"

"Thought we could go out and grab something to eat."

For some reason, her heart flopped over in her chest. "Go out and eat?"

Obviously mistaking her high-pitched response for fear, he softened his features. "I know this place. My brothers and I go there all the time. It'll be safe."

It was better if he thought she was afraid instead of knowing the truth. Which was what? The sudden increase in her heart rate was due to excitement? But that was silly. This wasn't a date.

Calmly, she placed the folded shirt on the dresser. "I don't have anything nice to wear."

"What you're wearing is fine," he replied, pushing out of the doorway. "It's not that kind of place. You game?"

Could she really say no? Smoothing her suddenly damp hands along her jeans, she forced a tight smile. "Yes."

He studied her a moment and then stepped aside, motioning her forward. As she walked past him, she *felt* his gaze drop. "I really like you in jeans."

She arched a brow as her lips twitched. "Do I even dare ask why?"

Heated cobalt eyes drifted slowly back to hers. A half grin appeared. "It has to do with how well those pockets cup your ass."

A laugh burst out of Alana, surprising her and apparently Chandler by the sudden sharpening of his gaze. She didn't know what it was. The teasing was beyond inappropriate, but something about him eased the frostiness of her exterior.

"You should do that more often," he said, following her down the hall.

"What?"

Chandler stepped around so he went down the stairs first. "Laugh."

She didn't respond to that. Waiting in the entryway while he grabbed the keys, she then followed him out to his truck. Once again, she noted the detailed and near-perfect landscaping surrounding the driveway and porch. One day she would like to buy a home with a yard.

"You're going to have to let me know who you hired to do your yard," she said once she was inside his truck. "It's beautiful."

He snorted. "Hired? I didn't hire anyone. I did it myself."

Her eyes widened. "You did?" She glanced out the

window, eyeing the trimmed bushes, the roses that were months away from blooming, the colorful early spring daisies that were straining toward the fading sun. "You're good with your hands."

"I am." His lips curled sensually.

Muscles low in her stomach tightened. He was damn good with his hands and his mouth and his tongue . . . She shifted in her seat, closing her eyes, but it was already too late. Heat unfurled in her veins. Daring a quick peek at Chandler, she knew he was fully aware of where her body had taken the conversation.

As he backed out of the driveway, he cast her an appreciative look that started at her lips and ended at her chest. His overt sexuality was far from oppressing; it turned her on and made her want more.

It's just two people getting off, she reminded herself, and she would be okay with that, but strangely, it made her feel empty.

She needed a distraction. "So you like to garden?"

He shrugged as his gaze flicked to the rearview mirror. "I like being outside and I guess I like making things. You know? Taking a barren patch of land and creating something out of it. And I'm good with plants somehow." A quick grin flashed across his face. "My brothers say I have a green thumb."

"I envy that," she admitted. "I can kill a cactus in less than two hours."

He laughed deeply, and she found her lips responding to the sound. "It's pretty hard to kill a cactus that quickly."

"Not if you're me." She glanced out the window,

watching the houses slowly bleed away, fading into businesses. "But I do want something like that one day."

"You plan on buying a house soon?"

"I would once I got settled."

He looked at her, and then his gaze went to the rearview mirror once more. "Then you're going to stay here?"

"I'd like to." Her thoughts turned wistful, something that wasn't common. "I'd like to have a . . . a home."

Chandler was quiet for a moment. "Didn't have much of that growing up, did you?"

She almost forgot what she'd admitted the first night at his house. Shifting in the seat, she dutifully studied her nails. A manicure would be nice. Not having a conversation like this would be great, but her mouth opened and she started blabbing.

"Mom was never home and if she was, she wasn't really there. She kind of ghosted through the house," she said, sighing. "We didn't stay in one apartment too long. She couldn't keep a job to save her life." *Or mine.* "Eventually I was sent to my grandmother's."

"And her house wasn't much of a home?"

Her gaze flicked to the red light they were stopped at. "Her house was . . . It was cold. I mean, she loved me and I think she was happy to have me around, but I also think she was done raising kids, you know? I was unexpected."

His jaw locked. "Unwanted?"

She sucked in a breath at the blunt question, but it was true. Her gram loved her, but she probably would've loved not having to raise her more.

Chandler placed his hand on her knee and squeezed. At

first, Alana wanted to knock it away, but all she could do was stare at the large male hand. Something warmed in her chest and now . . . now she wanted to put her hand over his.

"Totally understand where you're coming from," he said, squeezing again. "I think my brothers and I would be pretty bad off if it wasn't for Maddie's family."

She glanced at him, biting her lower lip. They did have that in common. Not the greatest thing to share. At another red light, his eyes met hers and it took a great effort to look away.

His hand was still on her knee.

She kind of liked it.

Time for another subject change. "Did you always want to be a bodyguard?"

Chandler gave a little half smile. "I don't do a lot of personal protection anymore. I run the business and only get hands-on in special cases." He winked at her, and damn if it wasn't sexy as hell.

"That didn't answer my question," she said, feeling her lips curve into a grin.

"I don't know." His hand slid an inch up her leg. "I always kind of did the whole . . . watching out for others thing—my brothers, Maddie, and her brother. Just something that came naturally to me."

"Just like playing ball is natural to Chad?"

"I guess. I was the only one who could really pick what I wanted to do. Chad always played ball, since he was old enough to pick one up. Chase was primed to take on our father's business, but me? Yeah, I could do whatever."

Interested, she looked at him. "Did you go to college?"

"I did. Are you surprised?"

"No." She knew he wasn't just all brawn, even though she liked to say that. "What did you study? Kicking ass?"

He laughed deeply, causing her grin to spread. "Honey, I didn't need to study that. I could teach those classes."

"Of course."

Grinning as he checked out the rearview mirror, he switched lanes. "I actually majored in computer science."

"Nerd," she teased.

"I'm a badass nerd," he corrected, sliding his thumb along the side of her thigh. "What about you? Always wanted to be a publicist to the misbehaved and spoiled rotten?"

Her gaze drifted to his hand. "I majored in communications, minored in sociology. I actually wanted to be a psychologist but realized I wouldn't have the patience for that." She laughed softly. "No big surprise there, right?"

"Never," he murmured.

"But I liked the idea of . . . of fixing things—people." She snuck another quick look at him. "Repairing them."

He was quiet for a moment. "Some people can't be repaired, though."

Alana thought of the senator. No shit. "Then I do my best to keep that a secret from the general public."

"You do a great job," he said, and the genuine quality to his tone surprised her. "I mean, hell, you wrangled in my brother, and that had to have taken a minor act of God."

She found herself blushing. "Thank . . . thank you."

"I don't think you hear that enough."

Nope. Being a publicist meant you didn't get patted on the back a lot, because when a publicist was successful, no one knew it was the publicist behind everything. It was a pretty thankless job, but she hadn't taken it for that reason.

She wet her lips. "You're . . . you're not like I thought you would be."

"What did you think I was?"

"I don't know." It was hard to put into words. "It's just that you've surprised me. That's all."

Chandler eased the truck out of traffic, pulling into a parking lot. "Well, we're here."

The restaurant definitely wasn't high-end, more like the chain type, but she was okay with that, comfortable with the chill atmosphere. She started to reach for the door handle.

"Wait," he said, and she twisted toward him.

When she opened her mouth, Chandler leaned in, closing the distance between them. She started to pull back, but his hand snaked around the nape of her neck, holding her in place. The kiss was soft . . . and it was sweet—sweeter than she'd ever thought he'd kiss, like she was a fragile slice of a treasure he was only starting to explore.

Chandler pulled back just enough that when he spoke, his lips brushed hers. "We're not having dinner alone."

It took a moment for that statement to make it through the haze left behind from the kiss. "We're not?"

His hand slid off the back of her neck, leaving tight shivers in its wake as he sat back, tugging the keys out of the ignition. "We're having dinner with Chase and Maddie."

Alana froze, her heart dropping to her knees. "What?"

"It's okay. Come on."

When she didn't move, he climbed out of the truck and

walked around to her side. Opening the door, he extended one large hand. A teasing grin appeared as he waited.

"We . . . we can't have dinner with them," she said.

His brows rose. "And why not?"

"Your family doesn't like me because of Chad." Her breath rose too quickly in her chest. "Why didn't you say something at your house? I would've told you no."

"And that's why I didn't tell you. I wanted you to come with me."

She gaped at him. "Why?"

"Why not?" he challenged.

It didn't make sense to her. Why would he want her to have dinner with his brother and Maddie? He was her bodyguard—a very inappropriate one, but whatever. This seemed like . . . like a real date.

He wiggled his fingers. "Are you scared, Alana?"

"What?" She snorted. "No."

"Then get out of the damn truck."

Her eyes narrowed on him. There wasn't much she could do right now unless she wanted to sit in a damn truck. Sighing, she knocked his hand out of the way and climbed out on her own.

Chandler laughed.

"Shut up," she grumbled.

Unperturbed, he draped his arm over her shoulder. "It's going to be cool. You'll have fun. And you'll like Maddie."

Alana didn't shrug his arm off, telling herself it was because he did a great job at blocking the chill in the air, but she halted at the door. "Are they okay with this?"

"Yes." He opened the door, motioning her in.

It didn't take too long to find Maddie and Chase seated in red booths to the right. Not when Chase all but hollered the moment Chandler reached the hostess station. Nervous and unsure of what she was doing here, she took a deep breath and faced the table.

She discovered two things pretty damn quickly as she followed Chandler to the booth.

The pictures of Madison Daniels that she'd unearthed while working with Chad hadn't done the petite blonde justice. The young woman was everything Alana wasn't— tiny, extraordinarily beautiful with all the blond waves and big eyes. From what she could see of the light sweater she wore, she sat and dressed with an innate elegance.

And lastly? By the look on Chase's face, they'd had no idea Chandler was bringing her along.

Man, she wanted to punch him in the stomach—or the balls—right about now.

The backs of her ears burned as Maddie's wide eyes bounced from Chandler to her and then to Chase as Chandler slid into the booth. Her body felt stiff as she sat, clenching her hands together in her lap.

"You know my brother." Chandler started the introductions. "This is Maddie. I don't think you two have met."

Calling on every ounce of professionalism in her, Alana extended a hand and smiled. "No. We haven't. It's nice to meet you."

Maddie shook her hand. "It's . . . um, really good to meet you, too."

The heat started to creep down the back of her neck. "You're feeling better?" When a look of confusion marred

137

Maddie's features, Alana squeezed her hands so tightly that her nails started to dig into her skin. "I was at Chandler's house Friday night when ginger ale and crackers were mentioned."

"Oh. Yes. That's right. Chase mentioned running into you." She smiled as she glanced at Chase. "Thank you. Just a quick stomach bug."

Alana nodded, at a loss as to what to say from this point. It was like she'd never worked with the public or in awkward situations before.

"What are you guys eating?" Chandler asked, eyeing the menu like the four of them ate together all the time.

Alana wasn't so hungry anymore.

"Steak," answered Chase, alternating between staring at Alana and gaping at his brother. "Hon?"

Maddie blinked once. "Chicken."

"What about you?" Chandler smiled at her, and her stupid Godforsaken heart spasmed.

She quickly glanced at the menu and went with a Cobb salad. Chandler scoffed at that, pushing for her to order something more, so she settled on a side order of fries.

The silence at the table was interrupted when the waitress appeared and took their orders, but that was only a slight reprieve.

Chase leaned back against the booth, folding his arms. His expression, the aloof coldness, reminded her of Chandler. "So you're staying in D.C. now?"

Picking at the edge of a napkin, she nodded. "I'm working at Images downtown."

"Oh," Maddie said. "That's not too far from the Smithsonian."

Sliding a long look at Chandler, Chase arched one dark eyebrow. "Have you talked to Chad yet?"

"Nope." Chandler picked up his glass, eyeing his brother over the rim.

Alana shifted uncomfortably, somehow forgetting until that moment that Bridget not only worked with Maddie but was also friends with her. How in the world that had slipped her mind was beyond her.

"I have," replied Chase.

Maddie's eyes widened as she fixed her gaze on the empty plate before her, and Alana wanted to crawl under the table.

"Yeah, I know." A muscle began to tick along Chandler's jaw.

Chase met his brother's stare. "Did you really think I wasn't going to tell him?"

"Do you think I care?"

Alana closed her eyes as she inhaled a soft breath. It took no leap of logic to know that Chase was talking about her and Chad was most likely not at all happy.

"Man, after all these years, you still can surprise me." Chase shook his head. "Pretty amazing talent."

"Chase," Maddie whispered.

She got Chase's dislike and discomfort with the current situation. If anything, the brothers were hugely protective of one another. The Gamble brothers circled their wagons around one another. When she was younger, she'd liked to imagine that she had an older brother who would be that defensive of her.

Stupid tears pricked the backs of her eyes.

Dinner was a huge mistake.

"Excuse me," she murmured. "I need to use the restroom."

When Chandler stood, her skin prickled as she slipped out of the booth. Forcing a smile that felt brittle, she quickly navigated the crowded tables and headed for the restroom, her chin tipped up and her spine straight. She knew that when gazes were cast her way, all anyone saw was a cool mask, but inside, everything was a maelstrom.

Alana didn't belong here.

When Chandler had woken up Saturday night to find her gone from her bed and then asleep on the couch downstairs, huddled into a tiny ball, he'd been more than pissed. Not only had it been freaking offensive, as if a couch were better suited than sleeping beside him, he'd been confused. He knew for a fact that Alana had enjoyed every second of what had transpired between them, and he also knew that most women would give their ovaries to have a guy who wanted to actually sleep with them after any type of sexual activity.

But oh no, not Alana.

She was not a typical woman.

It wasn't until late Sunday night that he realized why she had done that and why she'd spent the better part of the day avoiding him.

The woman was more skittish than a man when it came to commitment.

Not like sharing the same bed was professing undying love, but Alana had run, and like any predator, he was provoked to give chase, to win her over, which had given him the idea to accept Chase's invitation for dinner.

But now?

Chandler watched Alana disappear around the corner and then turned his attention to the fucker who sat across the table from him.

Maddie blinked several times, like she was coming out of a deep sleep. "That's Miss Gore? She looks . . . so different with her hair down and dressed . . ." She grimaced. "Anyway, she looks like she's my age. Never would've thought that."

He ignored her nervous ramblings. "Earmuffs, Maddie."

She scowled. "What? I'm not five."

"Fine." He leaned forward, dropping a heavy arm on the table. "You know, I expect this shit from Chad. He has a reason to be a little piss-head."

"Chad is our brother," retorted Chase. "Therefore *we* have a reason—"

"You don't have jack shit, Chase. She has nothing to do with you, and if I knew you were going to sit there and act like a dick, I wouldn't have came."

Chase met his brother's glare with his own. "You could've warned us."

"Why?" Fucker. "It's not like I'm bringing a murderer to dinner with me."

"No. You're just bringing the woman who made Chad's life a living hell and blackmailed Bridget to dinner with you." He laughed harshly. "My mistake."

It took everything not to smack the fucker upside his head, and the only reason he didn't was because of Maddie. "She made Chad's life a living hell by making him keep his dick in his pants for five seconds—sorry, Maddie."

She mumbled something under her breath, raising her hands in a gesture that said she wanted no part in this.

"Plus she cleaned up his image, and you and I both know he was seconds from losing his contract." His hand curled into a fist atop the table. "Oh, yeah and she is practically solely responsible for Bridget and Chad getting together, so let's talk about how she ruined his life."

Chase opened his mouth and then snapped it shut. Exactly. Chandler leaned back, breathing harshly through his nose. He tensed when his shit-for-brains brother opened his mouth again.

"What are you doing with her?" he asked.

"Is that any of your business?"

He stiffened. "Look, I'm just asking. She looked upset when she showed up at your house."

Chandler glanced in the direction Alana had disappeared. There was no sign of her yet, and he hoped he didn't have to go in there and drag her out.

Because he would.

"I'm helping her with some problems she's having," he said. "Her apartment was broken into, so she's staying with me for a little while. Right now, it would be nice if she didn't have to deal with your shit."

Chase's eyes widened a fraction of an inch. "Wait. She's hired you, and she's staying—"

He raised a hand. "That's all I'm saying, because the only thing you need to know is that I like her. That should be the only thing you give two fucks about, all right?"

His brother looked like the ghost of their mother just sat down at the table with them.

"Chase," Maddie said softly. "This isn't any of your business, but Chandler's right. If he likes her, that's all you need to know."

He took a deep breath. "Fine. Sure. Yep."

Chandler still wanted to punch his brother in the face and leave way before the check arrived. Maddie managed to draw Alana into conversation once she returned to the table, completely back in control, but he knew she hadn't recovered from earlier. And he also knew he hadn't mistaken the sheen of tears in her eyes, either, when she had gotten up to leave.

Chase at least had the decency to cast apologetic glances his way every couple of minutes.

The thing was, Chandler kind of surprised himself with what he'd said to Chase, but it was true. He did like Alana, and those feelings went beyond the physical. How deep, he wasn't sure, but he'd be damned if his jackass family sent her running.

When dinner wrapped up, he was happy to see Maddie give Alana a quick hug. He shot his brother a dirty look, one that was ignored as they exited the restaurant. But Chase actually shook Alana's hand when they all parted at the doors, which seemed like a big step.

Scanning the dark street, he dropped his arm over her shoulder and tucked her close to his side. Her shoulders were unnaturally stiff. "Sorry about that."

"About what?" She lifted her head, face impressively blank.

"You know what I'm talking about." They stopped at the passenger side of his truck. "For the way Chase acted at the beginning."

Jennifer L. Armentrout

Her shoulders rose in a slight shrug. "It's not a big deal. Are we going back to your place—"

Chandler cut her off by clasping her cheeks and kissing her sweet and soft lips. He caught her gasp of surprise with his tongue, deepening the kiss, tasting her. When he lifted his mouth from hers, her gaze was unfocused.

He smiled. "You didn't mess up his life. You made it better. Fuck. You gave him a life worth having. So for that, thank you."

Chapter Eleven

Thank you.

Those two words kept playing over and over.

Alana sat in her office, staring at the schedule on her computer screen but not really seeing anything beyond what her mind was focused on. Or the images her brain kept spewing out to her when she wasn't thinking about how he'd thanked her for giving Chad a life worth living.

Every so many minutes, the image of Chandler formed in her thoughts, completely naked. The man's body was made for daydreams. The way he stood before her, legs spread and arms to his sides, wholly aware of his effect on her. He was a masculine study in beauty. Even the rough-looking scar on his shoulder and the numerous nicks across his rippled stomach added to his appeal. And what hung between his thighs? Alana was no inexperienced virgin, but she could count on one hand how many men she'd been with. None of them lived up to the length and girth of Chandler. She doubted many men did.

And no man had ever tied her wrists together.

Her cheeks flushed as her pulse pounded between her thighs. There was no escaping the fact that she had been turned on by the act or that the dangerous thrill of being completely under someone else's control had goaded her along. It hadn't been the sole reason for wanting to return the pleasure, but . . . It didn't matter.

It couldn't matter.

After the situation with her psycho stalker was resolved, Chandler would slip out of her life like a ghost and if she fell any deeper into his seductive web, she would end up like her mother, fixated the rest of her life on unrequited love.

Unfortunately for her, there was more to Chandler than just his overwhelming sexual allure. He was incredibly charming when he wanted to be, always willing, if not eager, to engage in a verbal sparring match, and he seemed to get her in a way that most people never did. How important her job was to her and how even though her tactics were a bit hardcore, they worked and they *improved* people's lives.

After the disastrous dinner, he'd stopped on the way back to his house to pick up ice cream. They'd eaten it once they'd gotten to the house, and he'd talked to her, about everything and anything.

It had been so long since she'd just talked with anyone.

Biting down on her lip, she scrolled through her schedule. There were no meetings this week. Ruby was handling the media for a charity that Dick in a Box was participating in, but she had a feeling that she was going to be assigned a new client. A local high-priced prostitution ring had been busted over the weekend and rumor had it that several politicians and sports players were on the lists as clients. The phone at the office had been ringing off the hook. Damage-control time.

She smoothed a hand over her head and flipped her ponytail back over her shoulder. She had a stash of rubber bands and pins in her desk but hadn't pinned her hair up completely. It was strange feeling the weight of her hair.

A knock on her door drew her attention. "Come in."

The door opened and the first thing Alana saw was a bushel of roses. Not half a dozen or a dozen, it was a freaking *bushel* of velvety red petals and damp green stems, carefully arranged among baby's breath and placed in the largest glass vase she'd ever seen.

Her heart leaped into her throat as she started to rise. "Uh, I think you have the wrong office."

"Miss Gore?" the deliveryman asked, his young eyes peeking out from behind the enormous arrangement. "That's you, right? They told me it was this office."

She gaped. "That's me, but . . ."

"But these are for you." He headed toward her, placing them on the desk. "Careful. They're heavy."

Her eyes scanned the roses and tiny white flowers as she stood there in a stupor. She didn't see a card, but she hadn't realized that in time. The deliveryman was already gone.

Sitting down slowly, she stared at the magnificent, beautiful display of roses. This . . . this had to cost a pretty penny and she couldn't even fathom who'd sent them to her. Surely it could not be . . .

It was time to definitely get some fresh air.

Even though it was near lunch, she figured a quick walk to the coffee store two shops down would be perfect. Either that or sitting here staring at the roses, wondering if Chandler had sent them to her. Logically it had to be him, but why would he do that?

This weekend flashed through her thoughts.

Pushing to her feet, she grabbed her purse and headed out of the office. She looked for Ruby to see if she wanted to come, but she was currently MIA, and continued on her way. Once outside, she stopped and hated that the new habit she had was to check out all the surrounding areas before doing anything. It made her feel . . . paranoid to look for suspicious people.

Of course, there was no one and she made the quick trip to the coffee shop, ended up ordering an iced tea, and just as she turned, she was once again floored by spotting someone she never thought she'd ever see again.

Or at least hoped not.

Brent King, the aggressive dickhead that had hung around the actress she'd worked with was standing at one of the round tables by the window, fiddling with his phone. He hadn't seen her yet or maybe he had, but didn't recognize her.

Unease blossomed low in her belly. She knew he had ties to D.C., but seeing him here unnerved her, especially so close to her work. The first thing she needed to do when she saw Chandler was tell him about Brent.

Heading straight for the door like a speed-walker, she almost had her hand on the bar to push it open when she heard her name.

"Miss Gore?"

Fuck.

Squeezing her eyes shut, she toyed with the idea of ignoring him, but she exhaled loudly and faced him. For a moment she couldn't move or speak while he stared at her with open dislike. Before—before all the stalker crap—it wouldn't have bothered her, but a chill washed over her.

What if it was him? And she was standing right there?

Pulling herself together, she swallowed hard as she raised her chin. "Mr. King, I'm surprised to see you here."

A sneer appeared on his handsome face. "Why the fuck would you be surprised?" he responded, and she flinched, realizing people were starting to stare. "You got all up in my business before. You know I got family here."

She did, but that's what being polite got you. "Well, I can't say it's nice to see you, so . . . whatever." She twisted back to the door, but his words stopped her cold.

"I cannot wait to see you get what's coming to you."

Alana whipped back at him, her heart pounding in her chest. "What does that mean?"

He shrugged as he sauntered past her, toward the counter. He bumped her shoulder—knocked it hard. "Bitches like you always get what they deserve."

Several seconds passed as she stared at the back of his head as he went back to paying attention to his phone, then she spun and quickly got her ass back to her office, back to the bushel of roses.

Brent could've just been talking out of his ass. He'd always been mouthy, but what if it was a threat? A not so veiled threat? She should really call Chandler.

She was still staring at the roses when she heard Ruby's gasp from her open office door. "Holy crap, that's a lot of

149

roses," she said, hurrying closer to the desk to inspect them. Her wide eyes met Alana's. "Does this have anything to do with who's on his way up the elevator?"

Alana stiffened, half afraid. "Who's coming up the elevator?"

"One incredibly sexy Chandler Gamble."

Her eyes darted back to the roses. It was him—he'd sent the roses. Oh my God, she didn't know what to think, but her Godforsaken stupid heart started flipping in her chest even as sweat broke out across her palms and forehead, and really, she needed to be thinking about Brent. An urge to get up and race toward the stairwell was hard to overcome. The only reason she didn't was because that reaction would be hard to explain to Ruby.

"I thought you two were just friends," demanded Ruby, and then in a much lower voice, "hussy."

She shot Ruby a look a second before a broad, tall form filled her doorway. Her poor heart did a cartwheel as she gripped the edge of her desk. If her heart continued this way, she was going to have a heart attack.

Chandler looked amazing. No big surprise there.

His dark hair was down, falling in soft waves ending just above his shoulders. He was wearing an old AC/DC band shirt and the dark, worn material stretched against his shoulders and chest. There was a bulge under his shirt, along the lip. He was packing.

Packing? Listen to her. Since when did she turn gangsta? Her brain was fried, and the way the jeans he wore appeared to be cut to fit his body alone hadn't helped.

"What are you doing here?" She immediately winced at

how rude it came across and not just to her. And it was a stupid question. He was her bodyguard. Though he couldn't hang out in the office, he'd escorted her to work and she knew he'd been nearby all morning.

Ruby's gaze sharpened as she silently exited the room. On the other hand, Chandler look unfazed.

"I thought you'd like to do lunch today," he said, strolling up to her desk and the enormous set of roses.

It took her several seconds to respond. "Well, I haven't eaten yet, but you don't have to come—"

"You hired me as your bodyguard," he said, his voice low enough that it wouldn't be overheard. "Therefore, if you are going out in public, I need to be with you."

Her thoughts swam. After this weekend and now the roses, she seemed to have lost some brain cells. "I was just going to order in."

"No need now."

She curled her hands around the edge of her desk. "I went to get coffee earlier, and I ran into Brent King."

He'd been staring at the roses, but his sharp gaze swung back to her. "He's on your list. I've had a hell of time tracking that actress's friends down. Did he speak to you?"

Nodding, she told him about the exchange, and based on the way his eyes narrowed, it didn't look good. "Now that I know he's here, I'm going to run some searches." He glanced at the roses again, frowning slightly. "Nice flowers."

"They are." She flushed, realizing she hadn't thanked him for them, and that made her feel like something that rhymed with über-witch. "You didn't, um, have to send them, but thank you."

Chandler's icy blue gaze moved to hers.

She swallowed. "They're very beautiful, but I'm not sure why you'd send them. I mean, what happened between us? Well, I hired you for this job, and that's all it is." As Alana continued to ramble on, Chandler's brows inched up his forehead. She squirmed in her seat, hating how idiotic she sounded. "Anyway, thank you, but you shouldn't have."

A moment passed and then Chandler leaned over, putting his hands on her desk. She couldn't help but stare at those long fingers and remember how they'd felt inside her. Heat burned low in her belly.

Oh God, that was so not the direction her thoughts needed to go.

"First off," he began, his voice still calmly level. "What happened between us Saturday night didn't have anything to do with you hiring me. And guess what, it won't be the last time, either."

Her eyes narrowed as she opened her mouth. How dare he think he could just say that and it be true?

"And you damn well know it wasn't," he continued before she could say anything. "Secondly, do those flowers have a name on them?"

At the change of subject to somewhat safer topics, she glanced at the roses. "Well, no, but—"

"It would've had a note if they were from me." Lifting one hand, he cupped his fingers under her chin. Her skin tingled at his touch, but his next words were like setting a fire to her blood. "Probably something along the lines of how I couldn't wait to taste you again and I'm not talking about your mouth."

Her breath left her in a rush. No man ever spoke to her like that. And no person had ever been able to render her speechless.

"So the flowers weren't from me." He dropped his hand, but his mouth replaced his fingers a second later. "But I'm dying to know who sent them."

It happened so fast she didn't have a chance to pull away. At least that was what she was telling herself. His lips brushed her chin, as soft as one of the rose petals inches from them, and then his mouth was on hers, kissing her, working at the seam of her mouth until her lips parted, allowing him entry. He tasted of rich coffee and something else sinful and all him. A moan caught in her throat as he flicked the roof of her mouth.

"Fuck," he ground out, breaking the kiss and tearing himself away.

Left panting and scattered, she watched him stalk toward her door. Was he leaving? Nope. He shut the door and locked it, then faced her. The hunger in the tight line of his full, expressive lips and the heavily hooded look to his eyes stole her breath.

She stood, her legs weak. "Chandler, what are you doing?"

"No talking," he growled, prowling around the corner of her desk.

Her eyes widened as he pulled her chair back. "Excuse me? No talking? Who in the fuck—?"

His mouth was on hers once more, but this kiss . . . Good God, she'd never been kissed like this before. Thoughts of Brent King and random roses vanished in an instant. It was like he was staking a claim, marking her as his with his

Jennifer L. Armentrout

mouth and tongue. She had no idea how that was possible, but she felt claimed. Knew that she was. There was no fighting it, not when his tongue rolled over hers as he pulled her against him. She could feel his erection burning hot against her belly, pushing through layers of clothing.

Chandler broke off the intense, fiery kiss and framed her face. He placed feather-light kisses across her cheeks and over her forehead, fogging up her glasses. His hands slid down her sides and for a moment, she forgot where she was and her earlier concern about this happening again and what it would mean for her. Her pulse was racing as his lips found hers once more.

As if he was trying to drive her absolutely senseless, he upped his tactics, slipping his hands down the outside of her thighs, sending currents of heat through her.

"I am so fucking glad I convinced you to buy these skirts," he whispered against her swollen lips. "And you wore one today. Perfect."

Before she could question why it was perfect for today, his hands slipped over the bare skin of her thighs. Pantyhose were the work of the devil, so she'd always sworn them off. Feeling his hands roaming up to her hips, under her skirt, left her feeling warm and sultry. His fingers hooked around the fragile material of her panties.

A burst of laughter from somewhere outside her office startled her back into reality. "Chandler," she hissed, grabbing his wrists. "What are you doing?"

"What does it look like?" A wicked glint filled his blue eyes.

Her grip tightened. "We can't do this."

154

"We can." Easily breaking her hold, he tugged down her panties. A wide grin broke out across his face as she gasped. "And we will."

"Chandler!" she whispered, her heart pounding. How in the world had she ended up in this position?

He gripped her hips and lifted her up on her desk, her bare cheeks right on her desk calendar. She'd never be able to look at Monday through Sunday the same way again. Or her desk. Or her office. But then he had her panties off, slipping them into the pocket of his jeans with a wink.

Heat flooded her face. "Chandler, we really—"

"I'm hungry." He kissed her deeply, stealing away her protests.

"Then let's . . ." She cried out softly as his finger brushed through her wetness. "Then let's go get something . . . Oh God," she moaned as his finger slipped inside her. "We should go get something to eat."

"I'm about to." He sat in her chair and rolled himself right between her spread thighs, working her with his finger the entire time. "Except I want dessert first."

Dessert? Couldn't he just be into chocolate or ice cream like most people?

"This is so inappropriate," she murmured, but she made no attempt at stopping him.

He paused, his head level with the juncture above her thighs. "Oh, this is totally appropriate."

Before she could question his reasoning, he dipped his head. The very next second, his greedy mouth was on her, his fingers spreading her so his tongue slipped in deep. The first lick nearly had her crying out as she clutched the edges of the desk.

Everything was quickly spiraling out of control. She was at work for fuck's sake, in her office for her *public relations* job, and there was a man's face between her thighs and his tongue—

"Oh," she gasped as he sucked on the sensitive nub. "Chandler."

He growled against her, and her body coiled impossibly tight. Who was she kidding? Things weren't spiraling out of control. She was completely under his control. The realization was as frightening as it was thrilling and it nearly toppled her right over the edge.

Passion consumed her. It was too much, and in the same sense, not enough. She threw her head back as he delved deep with his tongue. Violent jolts of sheer pleasure coursed through her and she bit her lip, to the point that she tasted blood, to keep from crying out. Release shattered her as she surrendered to the pleasure, to his power and control.

When the tremors subsided, Alana was a weak heap on her desk. A huge part of her didn't even care that they had done that in her office. Right now, she didn't care about anything.

Unexpected late-morning orgasms were better than Valium.

Chandler rose, carefully tugging down her skirt. He lifted her off the desk, placing her on her feet. He held her to his chest, as if he knew there was a good chance her legs wouldn't hold her.

Pressing his lips to the corner of her mouth, he smiled devilishly. "That was the best damn dessert I've ever had."

Chandler knew the only reason Alana went along with him and let him pick the restaurant without arguing was because she was still rocking some major post-orgasmic bliss. Which was good, because he wanted to eat somewhere he knew the exact placement of all the exits, the staff, and the easiest route to get in and out of. One could never be too safe, especially with the sudden appearance of Brent King.

And he could admit the smug grin he wore had everything to do with him being the reason she was in the relatively easygoing mood. But as they waited for their food to arrive and after Alana had spoken about one of her clients, he wondered about the flowers and what Murray had said Saturday night. Was there an ex? Was there someone else?

His hand clenched into a fist atop the table at the thought of anyone else being with her. He so did not like the idea of that. Not at all. But then that left it potentially being someone like Brent, and that . . . yeah, that was worse.

Alana gave him the perfect opportunity when she asked about the status of the suspects she'd provided him. Telling her about William and Ms. Ward, he watched her intently. Disappointment pulled at the corners of her lips. He couldn't blame her for that. The quicker they figured out who was behind this, the better. This whole situation was out of her hands and he knew it was driving her control-loving ass crazy.

"We won't be able to talk to the actress until next week and we're still trying to track down her friends, but obviously one of them has just bumped his ass to the top of my list," he finished, pausing when their plates arrived. He let her get in a few bites of her salad before he jumped on the more important question. "So you don't know who the roses were from?"

She shook her head as she met his gaze. "No. I really thought they were from you. I mean, I have no idea who else could've sent them or had any reason to. So, yeah, that was sort of awkward."

Unease festered in his gut. Who would send that amount of flowers and not take credit? He believed her when she said she didn't know, but . . .

"Did you catch what flower shop they came from?" he asked.

"No." She sighed, stabbing a piece of grilled chicken with a vengeance. "He was in and out super fast, and I was busy staring at them . . ." Her eyes lit up. "But the front desk should have the info. Whenever someone is delivering something, they make him or her sign in."

"We need to get that info when we go back."

Her brows pinched and her tiny nose wrinkled. "Why? You don't think it has anything to do with the creep?" She seemed to come to the realization on her own, because her face paled and she placed her fork to the side. "Oh my God, you think it was him? That he sent me the flowers? That's so . . . so fucking creepy."

His lips twitched at the curse, but the smile quickly slipped away when he realized the topic had stolen her appetite. Part of him hated that he'd brought it up then, but it was too late to change that now and he did have a job to do.

Sexy fun times aside, Alana was a job, and he was forgetting that.

Sitting back, he rubbed at the scar along his shoulder. An odd feeling poured into his chest, making him want to crawl into the booth beside her and cradle her close, like he had wanted to at dinner last night. The feeling had a name. Tenderness?

Aw, shit.

She folded her napkin into a neat triangle. "Why would this person vandalize my car and my apartment, then send me roses? That doesn't make any sense."

"It doesn't." He took a sip of his water, watching her over the rim. "Not if it were a client."

Alana frowned. "It has to be a client."

"Does it?" Even with Brent being here, something about that didn't sit right with him.

Her lips, the very ones he'd been kissing not too long ago, parted, but the waitress stopped by with their check. Irritation pricked at his skin as he took care of the bill before Alana could. Her frown grew into a scowl.

"What's happening here is personal," he said, sitting back against the booth. "At least, that's what my experience is telling me."

Flipping the long length of her ponytail over her shoulder, she shook her head. "I think your experience isn't helping you here."

He shot her a dark look. "That's doubtful."

"Well, you're wrong." She reached for her purse and started to slide out of the booth. "I would know if it were someone personal, wouldn't I?"

159

"Maybe," he said, following her. The line of her shoulders was tense. Instinct grumbled at him. "But the roses? The ripping up of all your personal items? It sounds like an ex-boyfriend and not a ticked-off client."

Alana all but punched the door open and stepped out into the strong early afternoon sun. The streets were crowded and she was walking fast, but he caught up with her easily.

"In a hurry to get back to work?" he said, placing a hand on her lower back.

She glanced at him, her expression unreadable. "Yes."

He kept his hand on her, an intimate gesture that served two purposes. He'd be able to react if someone rushed her, and it also pacified his need to touch her, but it wasn't enough. He draped his arm over her shoulders, keeping her close to his side. "I need you to be honest with me, Alana. If it's something personal, it changes everything."

She held her purse close and squinted up at him, the movement forcing them to stop along the curb, near the busy intersection leading toward her office. "How so?" she demanded, her eyes flashing in those narrow slits. "A psycho is a psycho."

"Not really." He scanned the streets and then looked down at her, capturing her gaze. She was the first to look away, focusing her stare over his shoulder. The sudden feeling that there was something she wasn't telling him was hard to ignore. "Alana, when it's someone personal, it can be a hell of a lot more dangerous, you feel me?"

"Yeah, I *feel* you." She tucked a tiny strand that had escaped her ponytail behind her ear. "I'm not sure what you want me to say." A car horn blew, silencing her for a moment. "There isn't a man in my life. There hasn't been one for a while, especially not one who was this upset, and . . ." Giving a little shake of her head, she blew out a breath. "No. That's insane."

He drew her closer, farther into his body. "What? What are you—?"

Alana's mouth dropped open and whatever she said was lost in a rising, sudden tide of screams and hoarse shouts. He started to turn, to shield Alana as a gunshot rang out, surprisingly loud among the chaos. But small hands landed on his back, pushing him—pushing *him* aside. He stumbled off the curb. For a brief second, he was absolutely dumbfounded until a soft cry sent shards of ice down his spine.

Police officers swarmed out of nowhere, rushing through the stopped traffic, coming from behind them and in front of them, their dark blue uniforms almost black in the sunlight. They tackled a man to the ground as Chandler finally got his hands on Alana, circling an arm around her waist. Turning to her felt like he was moving in quicksand. He couldn't believe it. He refused to believe that she had *pushed him* out of the way.

"Alana, what in the hell . . . ?" He trailed off, his body turning to stone.

She stared up at him, her eyes wide and full of shock. In horrified silence, he watched the blood rapidly drain from her face and the light dull from her dark eyes. *No—no, no.* In a near panic, his gaze rushed over her, and his heart dropped clear out of his chest. A red stain appeared on her left shoulder, rapidly spreading along the breast of her tan suit jacket.

"Ouch," she whispered, lashes fluttering closed. Her body went limp in his arms.

"Alana!" he shouted, cradling her to his chest as he brought her down to the sidewalk. *No fucking way, this is not happening!* "Come on, baby, open your eyes."

A group was gathering around them, but he barely paid them any attention. Placing his hand on her shoulder, he winced as his fingers were immediately covered in her blood.

"Alana, open your goddamn eyes!"

But like usual, she didn't listen to him. She didn't open her eyes.

Chapter Twelve

There had only been three times in Chandler Gamble's life that he could say he'd tasted true fear. Once when Maddie was ten years old and had thrown herself off the top of one of those playground deathtraps to gain Chase's undivided attention. He'd really thought that the girl was going to break her neck as she came winging down to earth. Chase had broken her fall.

The second time had been when he'd come home from school one afternoon in December and found the typically quiet house too quiet. Something inside him had driven him upstairs, to his mother's bedroom. He'd found her cold and lifeless in her bed, still in her silk pajamas, a bottle of nearly empty prescription pills on the nightstand. Until he'd realized that there was nothing he could do to help her, that she was dead, he'd been scared out of his mind trying to make her breathe.

And as he held Alana's still body in his arms, he had felt the cold bite of fear for the third time in his life.

"This is an entirely fucked-up situation," Murray said from the doorway.

He didn't look up or even think about pulling his gaze

away from the still, pale form on the bed. He hadn't looked away since the nurse came out and asked if he was family. He'd told him that he was Alana's boyfriend. Knowing the damn spitfire, she'd be pissed over that, but he wasn't going to risk being shut out of the room.

And hell would freeze over before he let her wake up alone or with strangers.

Murray cleared his throat. "You doing okay? The nurse outside said it was basically a flesh wound. That she'd be okay."

That was the good news. The bullet had made a clean entry and exit. The scar would be minimal and she'd wake up soon and would be able to go home—home with him.

"She . . ." He cleared the strange lump from his throat. "She pushed me out of the way, Murray. What in the hell? It's my job to keep her safe, and she pushes me out of the way and takes a bullet."

Murray ambled over to the bed, staring down at the sleeping woman. A look of respect carved into his harsh features. "A bullet that would've surely smacked you in the back and done some damage."

"Yeah," he muttered, smoothing a hand down his jaw. He was still stunned, absolutely awed. "She pushed me out of the way."

"I know." Murray flashed a quick grin. "Guess there was a role reversal you were unaware of, huh?"

"No shit." He coughed out a dry laugh as he reached across the off-white blanket and carefully picked up her hand. He threaded his fingers through hers and squeezed gently. "I don't know if I should be thankful or pissed."

"Probably a little of both," he replied, staring at their joined hands. Chandler knew how it looked, but he didn't care. Not even when Murray made the next statement. "You've got feelings for her."

It wasn't a question, more like an observation, and Chandler wasn't one to bullshit. "Yeah, I do."

Saying that out loud wasn't an earth-shattering event. Neither was the fact that he hadn't known her for years. Perhaps he'd realized this would happen when she walked back into his life last week, and it had only been strengthened when she trembled in bliss in his arms. Now that she had risked her life for his, foolishly so, there was no denying the warmth building in his chest, encasing his heart. He wasn't sure what it meant, but he did know she meant something to him.

He expected Murray to make some smartass comment, but the man only nodded slowly and then said, "Kind of hard not to when the wee lady tossed herself in front of a bullet for you."

Chandler's lips twitched and he didn't point out that what had been brewing inside him had started before her Superwoman antics. His gaze dipped to where her hand rested in his. So small and delicate . . .

"You need anything from me?" Murray asked.

"Could you get her rental car from her office?" When the man nodded, Chandler sighed. "That's all I need."

Murray stopped at the door, running a hand over his clean-shaven skull. "She's one hell of a lady, isn't she?"

His response was immediate. "That she is."

Left alone, Chandler traveled his gaze to the tensed line

of her mouth and brows. Was she in pain? The docs had given her something and there'd be a prescription to take with them, but it must've not been doing much. He knew what a bullet wound felt like—no matter how minor, it burned like being stabbed with a hot poker.

He was unsure of how much time had passed before her nose wrinkled up and her lashes fluttered. It could've been minutes, but it felt like years to Chandler. She moaned softly, and he scooted closer, damn near tempted to climb into the bed with her.

"Alana?" he called. Her lashes fluttered open and she blinked until her eyes focused on his face. He felt his lips stretch into a tight smile. "Hey there, how are you feeling?"

"Like I . . ." She paused, wetting her lips. "Like I've been shot."

"Well, that sounds about right." He squeezed her hand and watched her gaze dip to where he held hers. "It was a flesh wound. Nothing too serious. You'll be able to go home with me in a few."

"Nothing serious?"

He liked that she didn't question the going-home-with-him part. "You passed out, probably from shock and pain."

She winced. "So embarrassing."

He grinned. "It's nothing to be embarrassed about."

Her chest rose with a deep breath and her brow wrinkled even further. "I . . . I wasn't even wearing my panties. You . . . took them."

A laugh burst from him and if he could've without hurting her, he would've scooped her up. "Yeah, but I don't think that was anyone's concern."

"I don't like the sight or smell of blood," she explained, and he was thrilled to see color pinked her cheeks. She drew in a breath and winced again as she looked at her bandaged shoulder. "Ow."

"How bad is the pain?" He started to rise, but her grip on his hand tightened. "I can get a nurse—"

"No. I'm fine. It's a dull ache, really. I want to sit up."

Sliding an arm around her uninjured shoulder, he helped her sit up and then hit the button on the bed so she was in a recline. "How's that?" he asked, sitting beside her legs. "Better?"

She nodded as her gaze went to the plastic cup of water. Leaning over, he grabbed the cup and held it to her lips. Must be the pain meds, because she didn't fight him on the assistance or when he smoothed his thumb under her lip, chasing away a tiny drop of water.

When she settled back, exhaustion pulled at her lush mouth. "What are they pumping through this IV?" Lifting her hand, she frowned. "I feel high."

Chandler chuckled as the muscles in his neck and shoulders finally started to relax. "Some really good stuff?"

"It is." She settled back against the flat pillow, eyeing where he still held her hand. For one of the first times in his life, he actually wanted to know what a woman was thinking. "Did they get the guy?"

And then his muscles tensed again. "Yeah, the cops got him the second after he fired off a round."

"Who was he? I didn't recognize him at all. Did he say why—"

"It's not our guy, Alana." Reaching over, he tugged the

167

blanket up, feeling like a nursemaid. "Basically, it was really a wrong place, wrong time kind of thing."

"What?"

He nodded, recounting what the officers had told him while Alana was being stitched up. "It was some douchebag who'd just robbed a store two blocks down. He took off on foot and the police think he was actually shooting at them. We just happened to be in the wrong place."

She stared at him for a moment and there was no hiding the disappointment filling her cloudy gaze. He understood it. Not like she wanted to get shot or have someone who hated her that much to do something so horrendous, but then at least it would be over.

This was nowhere near over.

"He could've killed you." Her face slipped into a wobbly scowl that was more cute than threatening. "And for what? Nothing?"

"Kill me?" Surprise radiated through me. "You were shot. Not me. Speaking of which, I'm *your* bodyguard, you little idiot. I'm supposed to protect you, not the other way around."

A wry grin twisted her lips. "If I didn't push you, you would've been hit in the back and I. . . ."

"And you what?"

She met his stare and then her gaze flitted away as she pressed her lips together. "So you almost got shot—"

"You *were* shot."

"Anyway," she murmured, waving her hand dismissively, as if taking a bullet wasn't a big deal. "We were shot at because we were standing in the wrong place? How fucking wrong is that?"

"Pretty wrong." He smiled. Some guys didn't like it when a woman cussed more than they did. Chandler loved it. He watched her lashes lower, fanning her cheeks. There had been something—something important—she was going to tell him before she'd been shot, but it could wait.

"Hey," he said quietly, smoothing his hand over her cool cheek.

Her lashes swept up and a winsome smile appeared on her lips. "Hey back."

Chandler bent his head, pressing a kiss to the corner of her lips. "If you ever do anything as stupid as that again, I will take you over my knee . . . but thank you. Thank you for most likely saving my life."

Alana's eyes were wide as he pulled back, and he knew in that moment, he had to be careful around her, because she was the kind of chick who could steal his heart.

Thing was, he wasn't sure he wanted to be careful.

There was a good chance that Alana might be more than a little high after the second dose of painkillers. She was feeling rather . . . okay with everything.

Okay with being stalked out of her vehicle and home. Okay with missing a half a day of work. Okay with being shot for no good reason. Okay with letting Chandler help undress and then dress her in one of his old shirts. And most surprisingly, okay with being stretched out in bed beside Chandler.

Staring at the ceiling, she wondered how her life had gone from painfully orderly with the exception of random hate mail to sleeping beside the shirtless, sexy—*and oh my*

God, he smells like soap, spice, man, and so good—brother of an ex-client while recovering from a bullet wound. Exactly when had her life veered in this direction? And why had she agreed to allow Chandler to scoop her up like it was their wedding night and carry her upstairs to bed—to *his* bed?

Oh, yes. It probably had something to do with the vroom-vroom Vicodin.

Chandler was asleep beside her, or at least she believed he was. His breathing was deep and even, and the warm arm pressed against her uninjured shoulder hadn't moved in a while. He was shirtless, of course, because why should he cover all those beautiful ropey muscles? Now they'd have matching scars on their shoulders. How cute.

She squeezed her eyes shut, mentally cursing her addled thoughts.

There was no way she could sleep like this. She was an on-her-side kind of gal and if she rolled onto her good side, then she'd be facing Chandler and . . . then came marriage and a baby carriage or something like that.

So far she'd been handling things pretty damn well. Only came close to a major breakdown when she got an eyeful of her apartment. Getting shot sort of felt like the tip of the fucked-up iceberg. Although she'd been nothing more than an innocent bystander, when she first woke up, all she could think was that someone hated her so badly that they shot her. Talk about an eye-opening experience. Had her tactics really been that bad? Hadn't she helped these people in the long run? Not all of them. In the silence of the dark room, she could admit that to herself. There were those on the fringes whose lives were changed after Alana took a case.

Sometimes it was friends, other times it was lovers or family, who had to be neatly cut out of the person's life to succeed. And she had done the cutting.

Did she regret it now? She couldn't, but maybe she could've been a little less harsh about things. Catch more bees with honey. Or was that bears? While she wanted this little ditty of self-realization to change things, it wouldn't. Her job, well, it was all that she had at the end of the day. This—whatever this was with Chandler—wouldn't be forever. She wasn't so stupid to believe in that, and she would never allow herself to fall into that trap.

But in the shocking seconds after she'd felt the searing pain in her shoulder, she had seen the horror in Chandler's gaze, the raw emotion that surprised her. He'd stared at her like he was facing the loss of something precious to him.

Glancing at the man beside her, she sighed. No matter how damn sexy and sinful that trap was, it was still a trap. Because when his job was complete and he grew bored with her, he'd leave and all she'd have was her job. Blowing out a breath, she squeezed her eyes shut and willed her brain to shut down and for her heart to stop racing.

A few seconds later, the arm between them lifted. "Come on." When she didn't move, he grumbled something under his breath. "I won't tell anyone."

Her lips curved up at the corners, but she still didn't move. Doing so may not seem like such a big deal to others, but to her it was a monumental step.

Also another nail in the coffin.

Chandler sighed. "Waiting."

And he was waiting for her. Arm in the air, face turned

to her. In the darkness, she felt his gaze searching hers out. Her body and the sometimes-treacherous muscle in her chest yearned to do so. Was there really any harm in it? Probably. And if she was being honest with herself, she wanted nothing more. Later, she could blame it on the pain pills.

Drawing in a deep breath, she decided she'd face the consequences later. Right now, this was what she needed and wanted. Easing onto her uninjured shoulder, she placed her head on the crook of Chandler's arm and sighed. The sound cracked as loud as thunder in the silence and she waited for him to make some smartass comment, but he didn't. His large hand landed on her hip and urged her closer. After a bit of wiggling, she was fitted to his side in a way that had her wondering if their two bodies were designed for this.

Definitely the pain pills talking now.

Moving her arm carefully, she placed her hand on his bare chest and closed her eyes. Several moments passed and then she felt his hand flatten along her hip. The weight was intimate and cozy and . . . suffocating.

No. She forced herself to take a breath. It wasn't suffocating at all. Truthfully, it was relaxing and nothing like the other times she'd attempted to do a little cuddling.

"Can I ask you a question?" she asked, staring at the moonlight.

"Anything."

Her heart sped up at his quick response. Chandler was . . . well, he was nothing she had expected.

"The scar on your shoulder? Were you shot?"

His thumb smoothed over her hip, and she liked the constant, idle motion. "Yes. About four years ago."

"How?" She winced, feeling awkward. "Sorry. That's none of my business."

"It's okay. I was doing a job in Chicago. A white-collar was about to turn state evidence and wanted security before he met with the police. Thought the guy was paranoid, but turned out, he wasn't." His chest moved in deep, slow breaths, the effect lulling. "When I was taking him to pick up his daughter at school, some bastard lit up the vehicle with gunfire. I took two bullets, but the client didn't get scratched."

"Christ." She lifted her head, staring down at him. The way he said it was like it was no big deal. "You could've died!"

"But I didn't." His lips tipped up at the corners. "You could've died today."

She was seriously trying not to think about that or why she had so readily pushed him out of the way. "I didn't, but you . . . you do this every day."

"What I do is my job." He moved his other hand, gently cupping her cheek. "It's not every day, and what I do doesn't come cheap."

They hadn't even talked price yet, but lying in bed together didn't seem like the right moment to bring it up. She let him guide her cheek back to his chest and his hand stayed on her cheek.

"Can I ask you a question?" he asked.

She tensed. "Yeah."

"You grew up with your grandmother, right? You've said some stuff about your mom, but what happened to her?"

Unease formed little knots in her stomach. Talking about her family was hard, but she'd already gone there with him, opened the door so to speak. "I moved in with my grandma when I was seven. It became apparent that Mom couldn't take care of me. She still visited, off and on, until I was thirteen, but then she . . ."

The hand on her hip started to move again. "What?"

"She died—overdosed." She closed her eyes. "Mom . . . well, she was in love with being in love, you know? Went from one guy to the next and each one was 'the one' and none of them ever worked out. But each time she met someone, she gave away a piece of herself until there was nothing left."

"I'm sorry."

She sighed. "Thank you. It's just . . . The thing is, I loved my mom. Even though she didn't raise me, whenever she came around, she was happy to see me. I kept thinking that maybe I could've done something to, I don't know, facilitate her need to love. That if I—"

"There was nothing you could've done differently," he said passionately. "Trust me, I know. There wasn't a damn thing my brothers or I could've done that changed where our parents ended up. They set their own futures. We were just along for the ride. Same with you. You had nothing to do with how your mom decided to live her life."

Besides the bullet wounds, they had more in common than Alana really ever realized. Both of them had parents who were too wrapped up in their own lives to pay attention to them. If anyone would understand where Alana was coming from, it would be Chandler.

"Thank you," she whispered.

The hand on her hip stilled. "For what?"

She didn't answer, unsure if she could put it into words. After a few minutes, Chandler started peppering her with questions and she found herself answering them with little reservation. How her grandmother always believed that Alana should've been born a man and because of her mother's chaotic life, she was obsessed with keeping things orderly. She told him about the night she got the tattoo.

"Does the rose mean anything to you?" he asked, and she could hear the grin in his words.

"No." She laughed softly. "It was just on TV that night and it reminded me of my mom. Like she had already started to wither, but if I could keep her in this protective vase, she would be okay."

"Sounds like the rose does mean something to you."

Her nose wrinkled. "Ah, good point."

Chandler switched topics, telling her how they'd spend the holidays at the Danielses' house and how everyone knew that little Maddie had been in love with Chase from the moment they crossed paths. She smiled at the childhood stories. It was obvious that Chandler had been the parental influence out of the three, getting the younger two out of trouble and basically taking care of them. It saddened her, because she feared that he hadn't had much of a childhood and probably wouldn't have had any if it hadn't been for Maddie's parents. Their home had been cold and sterile, but the boys had made the best of it and they supported one another above all else. Chase took over the family business, growing it in ways their father never could. Chad had used all those afternoons playing ball and turned it into a stellar career. And Chandler ended up doing what he had always done: taking care of others.

Mere minutes passed after the last word was spoken and she'd already begun to drift off. Unsure of whether she was dreaming or not, she felt Chandler's velvety soft lips brush her forehead, and she sank a little deeper into sleep and a little further into Chandler.

Chapter Thirteen

Chandler jerked awake, slow to process what exactly had woken him up. Wasn't his alarm or phone. The room was silent. Thin rays of early morning sunlight streamed through the blinds. Brushing the hair out of his face, he squinted and then reached out to find the warm body of—

The space beside him was empty.

He jackknifed off the bed, dropping his hands to where the pajama bottoms rested low on his hips. Son of a mother's tit, where in the hell was she? If she was sleeping on that goddamn couch downstairs, injured or not, he might strangle her.

Spinning around, he stalked out of the bedroom and started toward the stairs, when he stopped. It was barely audible, the soft cry, but he heard it coming from the extra bedroom he'd put Alana in. A huge knot formed in his stomach as he stepped forward, pushing the bedroom door open.

Alana was unaware of him. That much was certain. She was wearing pink lacy panties, and her hair fell forward in soft, dark waves as she got one arm through her white blouse. Did she think she was really going to work?

"What are you doing?"

Her chin rose as she turned to the door. A faint flush stained her cheeks, her eyes wide without the glasses. "Don't you know how to knock on a door?"

"It's my house."

Her lips turned down at the corners. "You still should knock!"

Walking into the room, he stopped a few feet from her and folded his arms. "Alana, you cannot be getting ready for work."

"Whatever," she muttered, turning around and giving him an eyeful of that perfect ass. His sex responded, swelling painfully. He tried to ignore it, because seriously, the hardness was fucking inappropriate at the moment.

He took a deep breath and inconspicuously adjusted his erection. "The doctors said you were off work until next Monday. You have a note. Your boss already knows not to expect you—"

"I feel okay," she answered, turning slightly. Her brow pinched, and there was a wrenching sensation in his chest as he watched her struggle to get her bandaged arm into her blouse.

She might feel better, but this was ridiculous. People who got shot didn't go to work the next day. Well, he had, but that was a different case. He stepped toward her, but she backpedaled.

"There's nothing wrong with taking a few days off and relaxing," he reasoned in a patient tone that even surprised him. "We can chill at the house, watch some bad movies, and—"

"No!" Her voice cracked on the word. "I *need* to go to work. I just got the job and even though Mr. Patricks says it's okay, I need to be there."

"You do not need to be there." As she started to button her blouse, covering the sweet swells lifted by the pink bra, he inched closer to her. "You need to be here."

Her fingers stopped and she lifted her gaze. "Here?"

The way she said that one word, like it was the most horrifying idea, was confusing and fucking irritating. Opening his mouth to point that out, he stopped when he watched her gaze dart from him to the door and back again, as if she were judging the distance. But to do what?

It hit him then with the force of a Mack truck.

Alana was *running*.

Running from him, and the reason why seemed ridiculous, but this woman had more commitment issues than his two brothers combined. She had slept beside him all night and he knew without a shadow of a doubt that it had been the first time for her. Something like that shouldn't be such a big deal, but it was to her.

A surge of male pride blasted him. It was wrong, considering how she was reacting now, but he'd been the first guy she'd slept beside and fuck if no one could take that from him.

He wasn't going to let her run. That shit stopped now. "You're staying here."

Anger flashed in her eyes, turning them nearly black. "Are you telling me what to do?"

"Yes." He flashed a quick grin. "Someone has to."

"No one needs to." Her hands dropped to her sides, balling into fists.

"I disagree. See, that's your problem. You've spent your whole life bossing people around and taking care of other people's lives." Pointing out that she also spent her life running from intimacy was so not a good idea right now. "That changes today. I'm telling you what to do and I'm going to take care of you."

Her mouth dropped open as she stared at him. Then she swallowed. "I don't know if I should be pissed off or flattered by that statement."

"I say we go with flattered."

Turning away, she lifted her arm and pressed her palm to her forehead. "I . . . I appreciate what you're trying to do, but I need to go to work."

"That's the last thing you need to do." He took another step, catching the scent of lilacs and vanilla. "Come on, don't fight me on this. Anything but this. You were shot yesterday, Alana. For crying out loud, let me take care of you."

Her chest rose swiftly. "Why . . . why would you want to?"

Had she really just asked that? "Why wouldn't I want to?"

As she watched him wryly, her lower lip trembled. It was the only real emotion she showed and for a moment, he thought she was going to cave, that the woman would finally listen to him, but then she shook her head and started reworking the buttons.

Reaching deep inside for a patience he didn't really have but seemed to grasp whenever he was around Alana, he crossed the distance between them, then stopped short when he saw the tiny drop glistening on her face.

Like someone had reached in and squeezed his heart, he closed his hands around empty air. "Alana, baby . . ."

She blinked rapidly as she backed away, hitting the edge of the bed. "No. I'm fine. I can go to work."

He was at a loss as to what to do, so all he could do was try to understand. "Why? Why do you have to do this?"

Her fingers shook as she lowered her hands. "Because it's my job."

"That's not a good enough reason."

Her throat worked and when she blinked again, her lashes were damp. "It's the only thing I have. Is that a good enough reason for you, Chandler? My job is it. There's nothing else and focusing on my job, well, that allows me not to really dwell on the fact that I have no one. I'm not like you. I don't have brothers and I don't have a surrogate family. I . . ." She broke off, the tears welling and spilling over her cheeks. Frustration pulled at her lips as she squeezed her eyes shut. "I don't know what else to say, and I don't want to think about this. I don't want to think about *anything*."

Chandler did the only thing he could think of in that moment, because all he wanted was for her to stop crying. Cupping her cheeks, he smoothed away the tears. Their eyes locked, and the flicker of arousal in her stare was greater than the distrust he also saw.

"You have me," he said, meaning it. The moment he said those words, he knew how true they were. She had him.

Her mouth opened, but he snaked an arm around her waist and carefully hauled her up against him and kissed her.

He kissed her in a way he'd never really kissed a woman before.

It was a sweet brush of lips and tender pressure, a kiss of reverence, and it shook him to the core. His hand shook as he smoothed his palm over her cheek, slowly deepening to the kiss. He expected her to fight him, but her lips parted and her tongue flicked over his first. His arousal surged hard and heavy, but he slowed it down, not wanting to hurt her or to send her running again.

But she wasn't running now.

Alana looped her uninjured arm around his neck, her hand delving deep in his hair, holding her to him. The kiss turned fiercer, harder, and it was all her.

"Stay here," he coaxed, letting his hand slip down, over the curve of her breast, to her hip. "Stay here and I'll make sure you don't think about anything."

Alana shuddered against him and her damp lashes lowered.

He kissed the corner of her lips. "Let me take care of you, Alana."

Her fingers tightened in his hair, causing sharp, delicious sparks of pain in his scalp. Yep, that turned him on. "Why?" she whispered against his mouth. "Why?"

"Because I want to." He pressed his lips to her temple. "It's as simple as that. I want to. And if you let me, you won't regret it. You won't think about a thing. I promise you."

She was silent and still and then she removed her hand from his hair. His stomach tightened and he prepared for another bout of fighting.

But she placed her cheek against his bare chest and let out a deep, troubled sigh. "Okay," she whispered. "Okay."

Not one to waste time, especially with this woman, he slid his arm under her knees and picked her up so that her injured shoulder wasn't placed against his chest. She didn't say anything, just turned her cheek farther into his chest.

His heart thumped heavily when he felt her lips pressed against his skin.

Oh yeah, she wasn't going to be doing any thinking any time soon.

Carrying her back to his bed, he laid her down gently. He hovered over her, his fingers lingering above the buttons on her blouse. "How is your shoulder?"

She stared up at him, her cheeks flushed. "It burns a little and is tender to move, but seriously, it's not bad."

"Good." He made quick work of the tiny buttons, parting the soft material. Sliding an arm under her back, he sat her up, and it did strange things to his heart when she rested against him. "Wait until you're healed. The things I want to do to you . . ."

He carefully removed the shirt from her shoulder, sliding it over the small bandage covering the patch of skin. Dropping the material aside, he reached around her, unhooked her bra, and placed a kiss to the side of her neck.

"Is this how you're going to take care of me?" she asked.

"One of the ways." Guiding her down, he leaned over her, soaking in the way she looked in his bed, only in her panties. She started to cover her chest, but he caught her arms, easing them back to her sides. "You're absolutely beautiful. No reason to hide yourself."

A flush traveled down her throat and over her chest. Her nipples tightened under the intensity of his gaze. He smiled and then dipped his head, flicking his tongue over each nipple before sucking one into his mouth. Her moan reverberated through his skull, an erotic cocktail that made his arousal almost painful.

Her hips shifted restlessly, drawing his attention. Grinning, he kissed his way down her belly, lapping and nipping as he went. By the time he pulled off her panties, she was ready for him. He licked into her sweet hotness, groaning at the taste of what he'd been craving since yesterday. Some men thought this was a chore, but with Alana, it was a fucking blessing. Delving in with his tongue, he watched her.

Her lips parted and her breasts rose and fell seductively. When his tongue circled her clit, her head fell back against the pillow and a soft, mewling moan escaped her rosy lips.

"Goddamn," he groaned, his eyes riveted to her face. His body ached to be inside her. There was a good chance he was going to lose it without even getting his pajama bottoms off. Release was burning through him, already on the brink of an orgasm. He'd never been this hot for a woman before. He'd never fucking cared this much.

The *L* word was forming in his thoughts, and what did ya know, it didn't freak him out. It didn't make him want to run for the hills screaming. On the other hand, it made him want to mark her, to claim her. It made him want to please her and to hear her say those words.

When had it started? He didn't know. Was it the moment she'd burst through the door at Leather and Lace or further back, when she'd come to the house the very first time? Or was it the first time she'd cried out, coming in his arms? It could've been on the ride to dinner afterward or in her office, her sweet ass up on her desk. Maybe it was when she'd opened her eyes in the hospital, concerned about not wearing panties? Last night, when she'd finally curled up against him? Or just now, when he'd walked in on her, finally seeing her vulnerable.

All of his brothers had fallen hard and fallen fast, so why would he be any different? Honestly, he didn't care what moment had made it happen.

Chandler slipped a finger in her wetness and was rewarded with a breathy moan. Taking deep breaths and putting the brakes on the way his hips unconsciously followed the movements of his fingers, he worked slowly. He was captivated by the flicker of emotions whirling across her face and drawn in by the way she rolled her hips, coaxing him deeper and faster.

"Please," she said. "Chandler, please."

Dropping between her thighs, he blew a hot breath over her clit, and she cried out. "I'm here, right here," he said.

Her breaths came out in pants. "No."

Chandler froze between her thighs. "No?"

"I don't want that," she said, eyes open and fixed on his face. "I want you."

"You have me."

A smile raced across her lips, full and absolutely dazzling. Luckiest man alive to be on the receiving end of something so fucking marvelous. "I want you *in* me."

Holy shit, had he heard her right? Like being handed a winning lottery ticket and not believing it. "Are you sure?"

Fuck. Listen to him. *Are you sure?*

She wet her lips, and he groaned. "Positive."

For a few second, he didn't move, and then he was up and off that bed faster than any man had ever moved, shucking off his bottoms even quicker. He reached into the nightstand and grabbed a foil wrapper, tossing it on the bed beside her.

A breathy laugh came from Alana. "Excited?"

"You have no idea."

Alana was beginning to get a good idea of how excited Chandler was as she eyed his thick, rigid erection as he rolled a condom on. Good God, he was huge and unbelievably hard, and she was also pretty sure that he was going to fuck every troublesome thought out of her head in a matter of seconds.

When she'd woken this morning, she had panicked. All the things she'd told him last night had felt like bitter ash on her tongue this morning. Never had she talked about her mother or anything with any man, but she had with Chandler, and even though she'd love to blame the pain pills, they weren't what had done it.

And never had she woken up next to a man before, either.

Walls she had built around her had cracked wide open, and as she'd lain there, gazing at Chandler as he slept, she'd let herself feel what was building inside her. The rush of emotions was nothing short of disastrous. God, she wanted him, and not just on a physical level. She wanted a tomorrow and a weekend. She wanted a next week and a next month. She wanted a future, and she had never wanted that before.

The swelling that had taken place in her chest had been too much. She'd panicked and raced from the bed, needing the familiar—her job—but Chandler, he'd done another thing that no one had ever been able to do.

He'd chased her down, caught her, and brought her back.

And now she was here, and she wasn't running.

Chandler swooped in, kissing her deeply, and bringing her back to the present. The taste of him lingered on her lips as he got his hands under her hips. As he sat back, he pulled her onto her knees, straddling him.

"Tell me if it hurts your shoulder," he said, cradling her hips. "Tell me anything, and I'll do whatever you want."

Her heart pounded at the words, at the feel of him prodding at her entrance. Air moved in and out of her throat too quickly for her to speak. He kissed her again, tasting her lips and her mouth.

"I've wanted this since the moment I first saw you," he said, running his hands down her front, cupping her breasts. "I would've kicked Chad's ass out of the house and fucked you right there in the foyer."

At those words, her body went wet and ready. "In the foyer?"

"Fuck yeah," he groaned against her parted lips. "I would've stripped those damn pants off you, flipped you onto your knees, and taken you from behind, my hands holding your breasts as I fucked you long and hard. When you're feeling better, I'm going to have to live out my fantasy."

Oh God . . . "Promise?"

"Cross my heart."

Need slammed into her core at the images of him taking her roughly on the floor. She reached down between them, gripping him and stroking the hard, hot length, and his hips punched forward.

"God," he moaned, pressing a fiery trail of kisses down

her neck. "You keep that up and I'm going to be inside you in two seconds."

"I'm not complaining." She moved her thumb over his head, delighted in the bead of moisture already forming there.

He chuckled deeply but gripped her hand, pulling her away. "I want to savor this." His gaze crawled over her face. "I want to give you a taste of what it will be like with me."

She shuddered as she ran her hands up his taut abs. "Is this not going to be like it normally will be?"

A wicked, downright sinful look appeared on his striking face, and she pulsed between her legs. "Oh, it will be like this, but there'll be other times when I'll want to tie you up again. You liked that last time, didn't you?"

"Yes," she whispered, closing her eyes.

He sucked her lower lip into his mouth, and her hips pressed down on his erection. "Say it again."

Breathless, she rotated her pelvis, wanting and needing him. "Yes."

"That's my girl." He skated a hand down between her breasts, over her quivering stomach to her bottom. A second later, his hand landed solidly on her ass, causing her body to jerk and for every part in her to clench up with need. "Yeah, you like that, too."

He smacked her ass again, and Alana cried out, her body and mind spinning. "Oh God . . ."

His hand came down once more, and she kissed him without any inhibition, unashamed at how wet and lush her body became in response to his teasing strikes.

"So we'll definitely be doing some of that." His hand

trailed over her bottom, soothing away the burn. "And then I'll take you against the wall. The floor. The kitchen counter. And this?" His finger slid between her cheeks, gently probing her.

Alana's eyes flew open as the pressure turned to a pleasure with a bite of pain. "Chandler . . ."

His eyes held a wealth of sensual promise. "Yeah, I can tell you're going to like that, too." His hand drifted away, curving over her hip. He tugged her up, over where his arousal stood out, proud and commanding. He gripped himself in his other hand, stroking himself slowly. "Tell me what you want."

"You." She placed her hands on his shoulders, ignoring the twinge of pain in her shoulder as she watched his hand move. In response, her body tightened.

"I think you can say it better."

Her gaze swung up and her eyes narrowed. "You."

Stroke up. Stroke down. "Better than that."

"I want . . ."

His large hand pumped. Chandler groaned as his back arched. "Come on, baby."

Her mouth watered as she rocked her body closer, feeling him slide through her wetness and then retreat.

"Naughty," he murmured, his grip tightening on her hip, adjusting her right above him. Just a thrust away. "Tell me."

She wanted to continue to push, but she was burning up on the inside. Then he shifted and his head pushed in. A spasm lashed through her and she tried to bear down, to take him fully, but he stilled her.

Alana wanted to punch the guy, but she wanted him inside her more. "I want *you*."

"That's all you ever have to say."

He thrust up, and Alana cried out as he entered her in one deep and long thrust of his hips. The pressure of him filling her was nearly overwhelming, and he held still as her body adjusted to his size.

"I've never felt something so . . ." He shook his head, eyes opening and fixing on hers. One hand curled around the back of her head, urging her down to his mouth. He kissed her, drawing her in as he moved his hips again. "You're fucking perfect."

Alana let those words wrap around her as she braced herself on her knees and started to slowly ride him, matching his thrusts. Pleasure coiled tightly as he withdrew and then eased his way back in. She'd never felt so full before. The slow pace picked up and his hips were pounding up into hers as she held onto his shoulders, matching him. Shards of pleasure hit her. She shouted out as the orgasm tore through her, deep and fast, and wholly shattering.

Her release was still rolling through her as Chandler unexpectedly lifted her. She whimpered at the loss of the fullness, but then he turned her around. In every movement, he was mindful of her shoulder while she had forgotten it. Bullet wound? Whatever. All she was focused on was the man now behind her, whispering things that scorched her cheeks and ears. The man was raw and primitive. He oozed sex and pleasure like most men breathed.

Chandler guided her so that her back was against his chest. He spread her thighs wide and seated himself deep inside her. She moaned at the fullness of the new position and then tensed when he cupped her breast, rolling her nipple and plucking until it ached deliciously. His other hand trailed down her stomach, his fingers easily finding the bundle of nerves at the juncture of her thighs, and then he started to move again.

"Oh God," she gasped, eyes wide, mouth parted.

The friction of him moving in and out, along with both his hands working her, was too much on her sensitive skin. She wanted him to stop, to speed up, and it was too much and yet never enough. The second time she came, he joined her. As he dropped his head against her uninjured shoulder, his thrusts became irregular, soul searing and deep. She pulsed and squeezed around him as he came, his hard muscles flexing against her back.

When the storm passed, she could feel his heart pounding just as quickly as hers. His lips brushed against her neck, so tender and sweet. "You okay?" he asked, voice husky.

"Yes." She was shaking, and as he eased out of her, she would've fallen flat on her face if he hadn't held onto her.

Chandler eased them down onto the bed, nestling her front to his chest, his hand on her bare hip. "Are you sure?"

Other than feeling absolutely boneless and like a useless pile of goo, she felt great. A sleepy smile tugged at her lips. "I'm sure."

He leaned over, kissing her softly, and as he pulled back, he pulled her closer so that their legs tangled together. "I could use a nap."

She giggled, not even embarrassed by the light sound. "We just got up."

"Yep. I still could use a nap."

Closing her eyes, she listened to his heart rate slow down. "Okay. Me, too."

"You're not going to make a mad dash for the other bedroom and lock yourself in?"

Her smile spread. "No."

One eye pried open. "You promise?"

"Promise."

192

Chapter Fourteen

Things weren't as awkward as Alana expected them to be the following morning. Wearing one of Chandler's old cotton shirts and nothing else, she sat on the stool in the kitchen while Chandler displayed another wonderful ability.

Frying bacon shirtless without managing to splatter grease all over that beautiful bare chest of his.

Alana nursed a cup of coffee while stealing long looks at the taut muscles stretching up and down his back as he flipped over the bacon. The sizzling and popping reminded her of what her brain cells had to have been doing last night.

Chandler turned, delivering a plate of bacon. "Eat up."

She waited until he'd joined her across the island. The bacon was the perfect level of crisp and when she bit down, she almost moaned.

Chandler grinned as he watched her. "Good, right?"

"Yes."

"The special touch? Brown sugar." He picked up a slice, and for a few minutes, they ate in companionable silence.

Alana had never done anything like this before. Have sex with a man, sleep with him, and then let him make her breakfast and share it together while she wore his clothes. This was all new.

And it was all so . . . all so good. As scary—hell, terrifying—as it was, she could see herself getting used to this.

Chandler finished off his plate, which consisted of half a pig's worth of bacon. As he pushed the plate away and folded his arms across the top of the island, the look on his face said things were about to get serious.

Alana's stomach tumbled. "What?"

"We need to get back to business," he said, and her stomach plummeted even more. Somehow—God, she was an idiot—she'd forgotten why she was here. Not because they were a normal male and female, but because she had hired him as her bodyguard. "Like I said before, I think this is something personal. We're barking up the wrong tree looking at clients."

Alana munched on her bacon, giving herself a few seconds to pull her head out of her vagina. "By personal, you're meaning . . . ?"

"Exes," he said, meeting her eyes. "Someone who has an intimate knowledge of you."

She shook her head. "I don't think that's it. In all my relationships, things never . . . Well, we never got to any point that would warrant this kind of . . ." She trailed off, and then it came again, the same thing she'd thought before she'd been shot. She shook her head once more, brows knitted together.

"What?" His lips thinned. "You have that look again. What are you thinking?"

Suddenly no longer hungry, she placed the last piece of bacon back on the plate. "It's just . . . It's stupid."

"Nothing you are thinking or could say is going to be stupid, Alana."

Her breath caught. "I did run into an ex the other day." Taking a deep breath, she told Chandler about how long they'd dated and how things ended. As she spoke, a dark and dangerous look took hold of his ruggedly handsome face. "But it can't be him."

"Why couldn't it be this Steven?"

"First off, he's engaged, and the breakup . . . Well, he didn't expect it, but he moved on." She picked up the last piece of bacon. "So he's obviously moved on. And secondly? I'm not the type of woman men obsess over."

His jaw seemed to come unhinged. "What?"

Her eyes rolled. "Look, I know there's not a certain type, because it really doesn't have anything to do with the woman. It's the man and all his issues. Whatever. But I've never been close in relationships."

"I'm the first man you've actually slept the entire night with." The smugness in his voice was hard to miss.

"He has no reason to be this—this angry with me," she said, wiping off the tips of her fingers with a napkin he handed over. "And he's moved on, so . . ."

Chandler rocked back on the stool, arms crossed. "Maybe I need to talk with him."

A tight smile appeared on Alana's lips as she imagined them talking. She doubted it would involve a lot of talking. Probably a lot of fists.

Unwanted and unexpected, a shiver coursed down her spine as her gaze locked onto the deep blue of Chandler's. There was a dark cloud there, shadowing his features. Her entire livelihood depended upon her uncanny knack at reading people and seeing through their BS, but could she be that far off when it came to something personal? That the culprit behind the letters, the vandalism, and the break-in was right in front of her?

Was she that far off?

It didn't matter how many times Chandler tasted her or slid deep inside her, it was never enough. He was addicted to her—to the way she moved against him, how her mouth brought him pleasure and then riled him up seconds later when she mouthed off, or the way she cried out his name as she came. He couldn't keep his hands off her, not when he was awake or asleep.

The days blurred together in a way that didn't concern Chandler.

In the mornings, he woke up beside her, amazed by how *right* that felt, and he knew that it was how his brothers must feel. It was nothing short of amazing for him to roll over, run his palm down the soft curves of the warm body beside him, and feel her push that tantalizing ass of hers back against his groin.

Every morning, he took her before he said his first word, and she was always, deliciously ready.

He'd slide into her from behind, hooking her leg over his. He took her in the mornings in a slow, languid pace that always quickly spiraled out of control, leaving both of them panting for breath and their hearts racing.

Then they would shower. Each time, Alana would argue that it would probably be more beneficial if they'd shower separately, but after one kiss, she'd relent. Water conservation aside, sex in the shower was never an easy feat, especially not with her shoulder, although it was healing nicely. He'd take her from behind or get down on his knees, bringing her to release with his mouth and fingers. Or they both would end up on the floor of the wide shower, her seated firmly in his lap, riding him and taking him in a way only Alana was capable of.

At some point, they'd eat breakfast. Sometimes in bed. Sometimes in the kitchen. Each time, it ended with him getting his favorite kind of dessert. And every night they went to bed, he couldn't stay out of her. Normally his sexual appetite ran on the kinky side of things, but with her shoulder, he found himself not wanting to risk it, and for the first time in many years, he didn't have a problem with vanilla sex. As long as he was wrapped in her slick hotness, he was in heaven, and the sex was more than enough to satisfy him. Until it was over and then he wanted her again. He always wanted her.

But it was more than the sex.

For the first time, Chandler found himself wanting her to talk to him, to tell him her thoughts, to share her memories, and to involve him in her life. Typically this would be the point in a relationship where he'd shut down or hightail his ass out of there, but like with the sex, he just couldn't get enough of her. It was the same with him. He shared things with her over the course of the week that only his brothers knew. What was between them had rapidly grown beyond a physical attraction and into something a hell of a lot stronger than "like" or casual.

Chandler wasn't sure at exactly what moment he'd fully

accepted that he'd fallen—and fallen like a fucking tree—
for Alana. What he was feeling in his chest and what he
wanted from her? It was love.

The most dangerous four-letter word.

Crazy thing was, his balls didn't shrivel up with the realization that he was *in* love with the stubborn,
commitment-phobic woman. He was pretty confident that
she felt the same way, but getting her to admit it wasn't
something he was going to be able to force. All he could do
was show her how he felt and prove to her that she felt the
same thing without causing her to run.

So he kept how he felt, verbally, to himself.

Murray had retrieved the mail from Alana's apartment
on Friday. There were two letters from the asshole stalking
her. Both vaguely threatening, warning that they would
meet soon. He didn't show Alana the letters. During the
time with him, the woman had finally begun to relax. Hell,
she was even wearing jeans more often. He didn't want to
take that away from her.

In spite of all the time he was spending with Alana and
how at the end of the day, he pretty much fucked himself
senseless, unease formed in his gut and grew with each
passing day. Whenever he was hired for a job, he always
knew who the enemy was, but with this? He was no closer
to finding out who was behind this than he'd been the first
day Alana walked back into his life. That little ditty nagged
at him, and from what information he'd gleaned from Alana
about her past relationships, none of them appeared to fit
the bill of psychopath. Then again, people who came across
as average and kind could be killers.

On Wednesday, he'd searched down two more on the list while Alana had napped in the living room. Neither of them had even remembered who Alana was, and he'd sensed honesty in their voices. By the end of the upcoming week, they'd be able to speak to the Jennifer chick, but he knew it would be a waste of time.

He wasn't putting his money on Steven, especially since the guy had moved on and Chandler had been able to track down Brent's connection to an uncle in the city—an uncle who hadn't see Brent in years. So if the fucker was here, he wasn't visiting the fam. Since then, the guy was a ghost.

Just to be sure about the Steven-fella, he'd gotten his phone number off her phone while she'd been resting earlier. The entire time he did it, he could easily picture her kicking his balls into his ass, but he needed that number. A quick call to Murray, a few detailed searches later, he got an address. He'd be making a visit real soon.

Her apartment had been cleaned up and what could be saved remained. He took it upon himself to get an alarm ordered, and it would be installed later this week, but even then, he wasn't going to be comfortable with her going back to that place until they knew who was behind this.

In two days, she would be going back to work and it would become dangerous once more for her. Protecting her without knowing exactly what he was protecting her from was damn near impossible.

And that realization made him desperate for her.

He found Alana in his kitchen, cleaning up after a dinner of Chinese takeout. He really didn't remember going to his room and grabbing one of the ties he never wore and putting it in his pocket, but as he walked up behind her as she stood at the sink, he was damn glad his perverted side liked to plan ahead.

Placing his hands on her hips, he tugged her bottom back against him as he bent his head, nuzzling the side of her neck. He smiled when she shivered and tipped her throat back, giving him more access. "Guess what?"

Her hands landed on his arm and her little nails dug into his flesh. "You want dessert now?"

Chandler chuckled. "Kind of."

Tilting her head to the side, she pouted. "I think I'm disappointed."

He caught that succulent bottom lip between his teeth and nipped. "I don't think you will be in a few moments."

Alana shuddered as his fingers slipped to the button on her jeans. Unhooking them, he nearly groaned at the tinny sound of the zipper and then tugged them down her shapely legs, along with her panties. Next, her shirt came off faster than the devil runs out of a church. No bra. Fucking A.

Cupping her breasts, he rolled her nipples between his fingers as he dipped his head, pressing a kiss to the small puckered skin on her shoulder. "Shouldn't you be wearing the bandage?"

"I don't think so," she said, voice husky. "It doesn't really hurt now."

"Hmm . . ." He kissed the angry little scar once more and then placed another kiss over her wildly beating pulse. "I like you like this."

"What?" She arched her back, thrusting her breasts into his hand.

He plucked her nipples, grinning when she gasped. "Standing naked in front of my sink."

A soft laugh lit up the kitchen. "Are your blinds closed?"

"Of course." He moved his hips against her rear, groaning in her ear. "If I saw you like this every fucking day, my life would be perfect."

"Every day?" Muscles tensed against him, and he cursed under his breath.

Not wanting to give her time to dwell and obsess over that comment, he curved his hand around her throat, guiding her head back, and kissed her. As he licked his way into her mouth, he pulled out the tie.

"Close your eyes."

She pulled back a little, brows lowering as she looked over her shoulder at him. "Why?"

He grinned. "Trust me. You're going to enjoy it."

A moment passed and then she exhaled roughly. Closing her eyes, she folded her arms under her breasts. "What are you up to?"

"You'll see. Keep them closed." Tying the blindfold around her head, he felt his cock jump at her soft inhale that followed. He likie. He likie a lot.

"Chandler?" Nervous excitement filled her voice as she lifted her hands, her fingers hovering at the edges of the blindfold.

He turned her around and his gaze moved over her body, smiling as the dusky rose tips of her breasts tightened. "You're beautiful."

"I'm completely naked and blindfolded, and you're dressed."

"True." He captured her next words with his mouth. He wouldn't be dressed for long. "You ready for me?"

She bit down on her lip, nodding slowly.

Gripping her hips, he lifted her up. Girl was damn smart. Wrapped her legs around his waist and blindly found his mouth. Taking her to the kitchen table, he sat her down. She squealed as her bottom hit the cool wood. Stepping back, he soaked in the sight of her. She gripped the edges of the table, her thighs spread, and he could see her glistening between her legs.

Something about the way she sat there in blind trust, mixed with the realization of how deeply his feelings ran for her, drove him wild. He wanted to drag this out, to slowly seduce her, but waiting would surely kill him.

"Chandler?" Her chest rose swiftly, and he groaned.

Tearing off his clothes, he went for her. Claiming her mouth in deep, wet kisses, moving down her throat, blazing a path to her breasts and lower still, where he got all up in her with his mouth and tongue. The taste of her drove him crazy, to the very brink. She came, her hips rocking against him, his name a throaty cry on her swollen lips.

Chandler's hands were shaking as he tugged her off the table, guiding her down to her knees. The beauty in what happened next was that he didn't need to say what he wanted. Threading his fingers through her hair, he moaned as her hot mouth closed around his cock.

She sucked—she sucked hard, taking him as deep as she could, running her tongue along the underside of his length as she cupped his balls, massaging them the way he'd showed her he liked.

"Oh fuck!" he groaned, hips pumping as she gave his balls a good squeeze. He didn't want to come like this. No, he wanted to be deep inside her.

He needed to be there.

Pulling himself away, he caught her by the arm and pulled her up. His body was shaking, his cock throbbing, as he flipped her around, bending her over the table. He spread her legs as he wrapped an arm under her, lifting her up onto her toes. Running a hand down her spine, he stopped just above the firm globes of her ass.

"I can't wait," he said, pressing against her until just the head of his cock parted her folds. "This is going to be rough."

She lifted her head. "I can take it."

A bolt of pure lust shot through him, and fuck if hearing that was like a beautiful chorus in his head. A guttural sound came from deep in his chest as he thrust forward, seating himself in her. She cried out at the deep penetration, arching her back. Sliding out a few inches, he repeated once and then again, in and out, until he couldn't take it anymore and lost all sense of rhythm. He slammed into her as he bent over, sealing his chest to her back. The table scratched across the floor and he dropped his hand from her back to her hips, his fingers digging in.

"Oh God," she moaned, moving back against him frantically. "Chandler!"

Her tight walls convulsed around him and that was it. All she wrote. He dropped his head to the nape of her neck, his hips pounding forward as his release exploded through him. Fuck, it wrecked him. *She* wrecked him.

An eternity passed before his legs felt strong enough to stand on their own. He pulled out of her and turned her around. After untying the tie, he held her close, wrapping his arms around her and pressing his forehead to hers.

She was trembling, eyes closed and hands balled into little fists against his chest.

Concern radiated from him. "Are you okay?"

Alana nodded but didn't speak.

His heart thundered in his chest. He had been rough. Fuck, they'd moved the heavy oak table a good foot. "Did I hurt you, Alana?"

"No!" Her eyes flew open. A faint flush stained her cheeks. "Quite the opposite. It's just that it was . . . wow. I think you screwed a few of my brain cells out of me."

Tipping his head back, he laughed. "Screwed a few brain cells out of you?"

"Yeah." She smiled as she peeked up at him through thick lashes. "I like it when you . . ."

He was already getting hard again. "When I what?"

She ducked her chin, adorably shy. "When you kind of lose control. I like it."

Oh fuck, he needed to be in her again. "I like it, too." Placing the tips of his fingers under her chin, he lifted her gaze to his. "And I love it when you lose control."

Her mouth opened, as if she was about to deny that, but he kissed her before she could deny what was so obvious. He wanted her upstairs and in *his* bed, but they got sidetracked on the stairs, and he ended up between her thighs, his arm along her back, taking the burn of the rocking motions.

Later, much later, they made it to his bedroom. Both of them were exhausted, and he felt like he'd run a marathon.

He lazily trailed a hand up and down her spine. Each time he reached the slight curve of her lower back, his fingers brushed the swell of her ass and she'd shiver. Of course, he kept doing it.

She nuzzled her cheek against his chest, letting out a content sigh. "What you did downstairs, on the table people eat at, wasn't very appropriate."

Chandler chuckled deeply. "What is it about you and appropriateness?"

Her lips curved up. "I'm constantly lecturing people on appropriate behavior, so I guess I've always felt like I should behave that way."

"Felt?" As in past tense. His brows rose.

She laughed. "Yeah, I don't think I could ever be appropriate with you."

His heart jolted like he'd slammed a shot of moonshine and he murmured, "Damn straight." And then he gathered her as close as he possibly could, making a silent promise that no one was going to get near her and hurt her again.

Chapter Fifteen

Alana woke Sunday, muscles sore in a pleasant way, and for the first time in many years, she wasn't looking forward to Monday morning. She wanted another week of Chandler and his fingers, his tongue, his mouth, and everything about him.

Smiling like a total goober, she rolled onto her side and into the spot Chandler had occupied minutes before. Stretching out, she smoothed her hand over the sheet. His cell phone had gone off, waking both of them. He hadn't answered. Instead, he . . . he'd made *love* to her, sweetly and slowly, bringing them both to a shattering climax.

The phone still rested on the nightstand, untouched.

Hopefully it wasn't an emergency, because Chandler was downstairs, making breakfast again. She should really get her lazy ass out of bed and take a shower, but her bones felt like jelly.

Mmm. Shower. She would never think of bathing the same way again.

A sudden knot of unease formed under her breast as she flopped onto her back. Her eyes were suddenly wide, fixed on the ceiling. She mentally tallied up the week—the sex, the conversations, the food.

Damn, Chandler could cook.

Nothing about what they had been doing was casual. Unless it was a one-week stand instead of a one-night stand. Or a one-job stand?

Smacking her hands over her face, she groaned. She'd barely spent any time thinking about what brought them back together. And that had to be pretty stupid. Someone out there wanted to scare her, maybe even hurt her, and all she'd been doing for the last week was getting screwed every which way from Sunday and playing house.

Instead of feeling regret, she felt a smidgen of satisfaction, and that alone made her feel a shit ton of dread.

She sat up, holding the sheet to her breasts as her gaze flickered around the room. The past week . . . well, it had been wonderful, but it had to come to an end. Her heart lurched painfully in her chest and the dread turned the blood in her veins to ice. When everything was said and done, where did it leave her and Chandler? Her heart wanted to say there'd be a future but her brain was telling her heart to shut the fuck up, because it wasn't as hopeful.

Climbing out of bed, she searched for her clothes before realizing she hadn't worn any into his bedroom in quite some time. Sighing, she picked up his shirt and slipped it over her head. A dull ache flared in her shoulder at the movement, easy to ignore, and by no means stronger than the feeling in her chest.

Now, after all these years and doing everything to avoid it, she finally knew how her mom felt when she—

"Stop," she said out loud, scrubbing her hands down her

face. Panic tasted like a bitter pill in the back of her throat. "You're not falling . . ."

Refusing to even finish that statement, she took several deep breaths and headed into the bathroom. Knots formed in her stomach when she picked up *her* toothbrush among *his* things. This . . . this was all so serious, but was it to him? To her?

Quickly brushing her teeth, she splashed water over her face and pulled it together. Her neurotic and über-idiotic tendencies were not going to insert themselves and make this happy, fun, and sexy twosome into a nightmarish foursome. Nobody had professed undying feelings for the other and no one was hurting. Everything was fine. It wasn't like her mom. She wasn't obsessed.

Picking up *her* brush, she quickly ran it through her hair, told herself to shut the fuck up, and placed it back on *his* sink.

She was downstairs and almost into the kitchen before she heard the voices.

"You haven't answered a single phone call of mine in, like, a week. What the fuck is up with that?"

Oh, shit.

Recognizing Chad's voice, she froze in the dining room. The door was right there, and a second later, she saw Chandler stride across the kitchen, shirtless, pajama bottoms hanging low, carrying a skillet.

Dear Lord, he looked hot carrying a skillet.

Okay. Focus. Prioritize. Chandler's hotness was not the concern right now. How to get back upstairs without being seen was.

"I've been busy," Chandler replied drily. "And I listened to your messages. There wasn't anything important. Not like it had to do with your wedding or anything. No one was dying."

"No shit, jackass." Chad came into view, leaning against the kitchen—oh God, the kitchen table.

Images of what they'd done on that table assaulted Alana's brain. She needed to get out of here, but she was rooted to the spot. One wrong noise and Chad would see her in his brother's clothes and well, that shit would be awkward.

"You haven't even been answering Chase's calls." Accusation rang in Chad's tone, and Alana frowned. "And you really should've."

"Why?" Chandler appeared, stopping in front of his brother, folding his thick arms. Standing side by side, Chandler was the brawnier and bigger of the two, but it was easy to see the resemblance. The same dark hair, but Chad's was shorter, messy, and spikey. Their profile was nearly identical—broad cheekbones, strong jaw. "Let me guess? He's like you and doesn't know when to mind his own business?"

Chad cocked his head to the side. "You're our brother, and therefore it is our business."

"Bullshit."

"That's how you treated us."

"When you were sixteen fucking years old." There was no real heat in Chandler's words, but Alana felt like an interloper.

Well, duh, she was, and she really needed to get her ass out of there.

"Technicalities." Chad flashed the grin that had women across the nation dropping their panties, even though he was now only concerned about one woman's panties. The baseball player sighed. "Man, something is definitely going on. Chase said you weren't over for card night—"

"Aw, do the whittle boys miss their big brother?"

"Maybe."

Chandler smirked. "Sometimes I think you two have fully functioning vaginas."

Alana pressed her lips together.

"Fuck you." Chad stretched out his legs, crossing his ankles. "You really should talk to Chase."

Chandler sighed. "Look, what I'm doing is none—"

"Maddie's pregnant, you asshole."

Alana's mouth dropped open at the same exact second that Chandler's did. He stepped back and only half of him was in view. His arms dropped to his sides. "No shit?"

"Yeah, that's why he's been calling you. Wanted to share the good news and shit." Chad smacked his palms off the table. A small grin appeared. "Her parents are going to *kill* him, being that they aren't even engaged yet."

"Chase has the ring picked out. You know that. He's waiting for the right moment or something." There was a pause. "Guess he waited too long."

"Yeah, but do they know that?" Chad laughed. "I must admit, I am so looking forward to witnessing that conversation with Mr. Daniels."

"He's going to eat Chase alive."

"Yep." Chad was grinning.

Another stretch of silence. "Man, when Chase was over

here last, he said he thought Maddie had the flu. Wow. This is . . . I don't even know what to say." Surprise and genuine happiness filled Chandler's voice. "Chase is going to be a dad?"

"We're going to be uncles."

"Uncle?" Chandler chuckled. "Man, that's pretty damn awesome."

Standing there, listening to things she had no business listening to, Alana felt this . . . this deep stirring in her chest and this urge to join the guys, to congratulate them and to wrap her arms around Chandler. She wanted to be a part of the happiness, because she wanted to *share* it with him.

Oh God.

There was no denying what she was feeling.

Blood quickly drained out of her face. The walls around her seemed to move in, crowding her. The ceiling had to have dropped several feet, because she felt like she couldn't stand straight. Pressure clamped down on her chest. Was she having a heart attack? Oh no, it was something far worse than that.

She was in love with Chandler Gamble.

Absolutely fucking thrilled for his youngest brother, Chandler stood there grinning like a goddamn fool. Chase was going to be a dad? He was going to be an uncle? No shit. Better be having a little boy. If it was a little girl, no male had an ice cube's chance in hell at getting past the three of them.

Chad looked like he was about to jump topics again when what sounded like a chair in the dining room deciding to mate with the table drew their attention.

They turned at the same time.

Alana stood a few feet back from the table, her face as red as a fire truck and her eyes wide. His gaze dropped, and he swallowed a groan. Damn if he didn't love seeing her in his clothes.

However, he did not like the idea of Chad seeing her practically naked.

And he really wasn't ready to talk to his brothers about Alana, which was why he'd been spending the week pretending no one was home when they called. It was obvious his two brothers were gossiping like two old nursing home patients, and Alana, well, she was way too personal and important to him to expose her to these two jerks.

Chad's eyes grew as big as a kid's on Christmas morning. He stared at Alana like he'd never seen her before. And he'd never seen his ex-publicist like *this* before. If he had, Bridget was going to end up a very unhappy newlywed, because Chandler would cut off his brother's dick. Chad slowly faced Chandler. "What in the hell is going on here?"

He folded his arms again, giving his brother the "don't fuck with me" look. "What do you think is going on?"

"Oh, I have a damn good visual, but I'm praying I'm wrong on that."

Anger pricked at Chandler's skin, and he had to tell himself that this was his brother, so it wouldn't be *appropriate* to thump his ass. "Be careful what you say next," he warned in a low voice. "I'm not fucking with you."

An incredulous look crossed Chad's expression as he pushed away from the table, glancing into the dining room. "That's fucking Miss Gore."

His hands closed into fists. "Chad . . ."

"I'm sure you haven't forgotten that every time she came around me, I felt the need to cup my balls. Or the fact that she blackmailed Bridget. Or that she's more evil than fucking Medusa on her period?"

That was it. He was going to knock his ungrateful asshole brother out, and he was a half a second away from doing it when Alana's voice stopped him.

"Your balls were always safe around me," she said, her voice tight as she leveled a cool stare at Chad. To anyone else, she looked unaffected, but Chandler caught the slight tremor in her lower lip and the stiffness in the way she held herself. "Please tell Chase congratulations. I'm sorry to intrude."

Chandler watched her turn and walk out of the room. Wanting to go after her but needing to handle something else first, he squared off with his brother. He cocked back his arm. Fist say hello to jaw.

Chad spun sideways, catching himself on the table. "Jesus." He straightened, clutching his jaw. "What the fuck was that for?"

"Are you really that fucking stupid that you have to ask that question?" Chandler seethed. Had the idiot been hit in the head with too many fastballs? "Look, I get that she doesn't make you warm and fuzzy, but pull your head out of your ass. Yeah, she blackmailed your girl. Total bitch move. I agree." He got right up in Chad's face, forcing him to hold eye contact. "But if it wasn't for Alana— No, shut the fuck up. I am not finished. If it weren't for her, there wouldn't be a Bridget. You'd still be fucking around with

God knows who. And if Alana hadn't forced Bridget to go out with you, you know damn well she wouldn't have."

"Well, that was sort of insulting."

"It's the truth." He forced himself back a step before he hit him again. "You have Alana to thank and instead you treat her like she's a terrorist. That shit stops now. She deserves your fucking gratitude and your respect. And a big ole fucking thank-you for the wife-to-be and the new multi-million-dollar contract your happy ass just signed."

Chad's jaw worked as he shook his head. "I get what you're saying and yeah, I'm acting like an ass. But—"

"But?"

"Yes." His eyes flashed with anger. "She embarrassed Bridget. She made her feel like scum and even though forcing her into that mess with me did work out in our benefit, I have a hard time getting over how she acted toward Bridget."

Chandler couldn't argue that Alana didn't have the greatest skills when it came to dealing with people, but how Chad treated her wasn't right.

"Are you sleeping with her? Shit. That's a stupid question. She was wearing your shirt. I think I got you that one for Christmas."

"Shut up, Chad."

Chad never knew when to shut up. "Do you have feelings for her? Holy shit, you have—"

"She took a bullet for me, you fuckwad, so how about shutting the fuck up."

His brother stopped yapping, his eyes narrowing. "What do you mean?"

Half tempted to just kick him out of the house, he picked

up the skillet from the island and told Chad what had happened last Monday. The tiny gleam of respect that was suddenly in Chad's eyes only made Chandler not want to hit him upside the head with the skillet.

"Damn." Chad rubbed a spot over his chest. "I don't know what to say. It's just that . . ."

"You don't need to say anything," he grumbled, returning to the stove. "So unless you want to piss me off more, I'm gonna make breakfast."

"I'm not invited?"

He cast a dark look over his shoulder.

Chad backed away slowly. "Fine. I'm sorry. You're right. I'm being a dick."

"I'm not the one you need to be saying that to."

His brother was just as stubborn as he was, and while he knew Chad was sincere in his apology, he didn't foresee him saying it to Alana any time soon. His brother left shortly after that, leaving his gut churning. He slammed the skillet down on the stove, irritated. His brothers needed to get used to Alana, because she wasn't going anywhere.

Chapter Sixteen

The burn in the back of Alana's throat told her that she needed to get out of here. While Chad's words and his attitude toward her didn't come as a surprise, it still stung. Made worse by the fact that she was pretty sure she heard Chandler's fist hitting Chad. The last thing she wanted was to create any strife between the brothers.

Shuffling into the bedroom she was supposed to be staying in, she stopped by the bed she had barely slept in. Her heart thumped against her ribs as she turned, tucking her hair back behind her ears.

God, Chandler had sounded so happy to be an uncle. In her mind, it was easy to picture him holding a baby. He'd be great as a father. She knew it.

This . . . this had gone too far.

Going back to her apartment wasn't safe, and she wasn't stupid. Okay, obviously she wasn't the brightest because she was in this situation in the first place. She needed to go to a hotel and then what? Find someone else to protect her and make sure the crazy didn't spread toward her job? The idea of bringing someone else into this felt like needles on her skin, but she had to get away.

She was close to sitting down on her bed and indulging in some really ugly crying, but she forced her legs to remain straight.

The scent of Chandler clung to her skin, even as she pulled the shirt off over her head and dropped it on the floor. Heading into the bathroom, she turned on the shower and cranked up the heat.

Her heart felt heavy as she stepped under the showerhead and the steady stream pelted her. For some reason, her skin felt raw and bruised, too sensitive. She shifted slowly, letting the spray hit her back.

She was in love.

She had gone and done it after swearing she'd never become her mother. Because wasn't this how it had started for her? Alana really didn't know, but what was between her and Chandler had gone beyond sex and a good time. It had morphed into a burning passion that knotted in her chest.

The truth was, no matter how she felt about Chandler, she didn't belong with him, and his brothers would never accept her. Chad's appearance served as a brutal, much-needed wakeup call.

Alana needed to get out before she got even more invested, which seemed stupid, because how much more invested could she get?

Closing her eyes, she tipped her head back and let the water and steam do its thing, wishing it could wash away Chandler's presence as well as it did his scent, but that was foolish, wasn't it?

This was a good thing, though, she told herself. Tomorrow

she would be going back to work, back to reality. She still had her job. She still had that.

Alana wasn't sure exactly how she knew she wasn't alone. The door to the bathroom hadn't creaked when it opened and she hadn't been aware of the glass doors sliding, but she knew Chandler was there before she even opened her eyes.

He stood there, still shirtless, and his pants were hanging indecently low on his hips. His gaze traveled hungrily over her body, staying in some areas longer than others. The way her body responded ticked her off. Her nipples hardened under his greedy stare and liquid fire flooded her veins. Air sawed in and out of her lips slowly as his gaze finally settled back on hers.

Feeling incredibly vulnerable, which seemed kind of pointless at this moment, she folded her arms over her breasts. She had no idea what to say. Being naked in the shower did not make it easy for casual conversation.

"You shouldn't hide yourself. You're absolutely beautiful."

His words created a nest of butterflies in her belly, but she kept her arms crossed. "Congratulations," she blurted out, and then flushed at how random it came across.

His brows rose.

"For Maddie's pregnancy. That's such good news." Her nails bit into her arms. "I'm really happy for all of you."

"It is great news. Chase will make a wonderful father." He leaned against the shower wall, seemingly oblivious to the spray. She wasn't. Her eyes followed the trail of water down his chest, over his tight abs. "But I didn't come up here to talk about that."

218

Her chest spasmed. "You didn't?"

He shook his head. "What Chad said downstairs was wrong. Without you, he wouldn't be marrying her, and he knows that. I want you to know that he apologized."

While she knew Chandler meant well by telling her this, she doubted Chad apologized before the punch in the face. "It's okay."

"No. It's not."

Having no idea how to respond to that, she turned around slowly, letting the hot spray of water wash over her face. Her skin pricked with awareness. "I don't want to talk."

"Is that an invitation?"

It shouldn't be. God knew continuing to cross that line with him wasn't smart. Her body and heart were at war with her head. She should tell him to leave, pack up herself, and get the hell out of here, but . . .

But what was one more time? One more night? It wouldn't change the outcome, staying wouldn't harshen the blow that was sure to come. It just wasn't smart. Then again, she hadn't been smart about any of this and look where she was? There was already an ache deep in her chest.

"Alana . . ."

The sound of her name on his lips sealed the deal. It was truly that seductive. He rolled her name around his tongue like he was tasting it. Looking over her shoulder at him, she drew in a shallow breath. "It is."

Chandler stared at her for what felt like forever and then he had his pants off in record time. His arousal jutted out proudly, hard and thick, and molten lava filled in her belly.

He stepped into the shower, closing the door behind him.

His hands landed on her hips and when he spoke, his voice whispered in her ear. "I know what you're thinking."

Alana shuddered. "You do?"

"Yes." He kissed the scar on her shoulder, causing her heart to squeeze at the tender action. "You're going to run."

She stiffened, her arms clamped close to her chest. "I don't . . . don't know what you're talking about."

"You're a shitty liar." He turned her around and reached between them, wrapping his hands around her wrists. He backed her up until she was flush with the cold tile. "You have that look in your eyes. Never really seen it before—the whole deer-in-the-headlights look. But you have it. You're going to run."

"You need to get your eyes checked, then."

"Smartass," he murmured. "Still a shitty liar. And you know what? That's okay." He transferred her wrists to one hand and placed his free hand on her hip. Tipping their foreheads together, he breathed in deeply. "Run if it makes you feel better and helps you sleep at night. It's not the worst possible thing you could do."

Alana wanted to deny it, because the accusation, no matter how spot-on it was, made her feel weak.

"So run. I don't mind." His lips blazed a path over her cheek and his teeth sank into her earlobe, causing her to moan. "I like to chase, Alana."

A bolt of red-hot lust slammed from her pulse and straight to her belly. "I don't like to be chased."

"You will when it's me." He slowly lifted her joined hands above her head as he slid his free hand over the curve of her rear, lifting her up until she was on the tips of her toes. "I will chase you. And I will catch you."

Chandler pressed forward, his erection firmly against her stomach. It felt like he was crushing her, or at least that was how it seemed for a panicked second. Raw emotions poured into her chest. She should push him away, stop this, but she tipped her head against the wall and her hips moved in slow circles.

"What's between us isn't casual." His hot breath caressed her cheeks, sending shivers down her, and then moved down her throat again. "And you know that just as well as I do. You just don't want to admit it."

"No," she whispered.

"Yes." His voice was raw, sexy, and pure sin. "Look at you. You can't wait for me to get inside of you."

It was true. She was wet, ready, and her hips kept moving against him. Already she could feel him inside her and it was a desire that was like a drug—an obsession.

Her eyes flew open as icy panic balled in her chest. "It's not—"

His mouth was on her, the kiss rugged and rough. Sparks flew from deep inside her and his tongue swept in, silencing the breathy moan building. Everything was spiraling out of control. Hell, it was already out of control.

Chandler rocked against her as he lifted his head, lips brushing hers as he spoke. "Don't you feel it?" He pressed his lips to the side of her neck, lapping with his tongue. "I know you do."

Alana shuddered. Her entire body was one giant pulse point. She ached for him, but the ache ran deep, blooming in her chest. He shifted his hips again as his lips roamed over her heated skin and she arched against him. Her body made her as transparent as a window and there was absolutely nothing she could do about it.

The combination of her fear and desire held a frightening level of power. Heat pooled between her thighs and her very being burned for him. Her head swam as he captured her lips again. His fingers tightened on her bottom, squeezing her as his tongue flicked over the rough of her mouth.

Chandler was . . . God, he was something beyond words.

Lifting her off her feet, he pushed her thighs apart. She gasped as she felt him against her thigh, so hot and hard. She was close to begging him, but he didn't make her wait long. Oh no, he hooked her legs around his hips, lining her up with his erection.

"Look at me," he ordered in a gruff voice.

Alana wanted to deny him, but her eyes opened of their own accord. His raw gaze stole her breath. In his stare . . . No, she couldn't be seeing what she thought she was. They barely knew each other. His family hated her. He was hired to protect her, but . . .

She suddenly wanted to cry.

Not breaking contact, he thrust inside her, deep and hard, and he remained there, seated to the hilt. There was no escaping him, and in that moment, it was the last thing she ever wanted to do.

"Feel me?" he breathed, nipping at her lower lip.

Alana felt him in every part of her. Then he started to move and her world fell apart. Her body arched into him and she kicked her head back. The piercing moan sent Chandler into a frenzy of action.

Each thrust slid her up the wall and then back down on his length. She couldn't move in this position. He had complete control. Her arms were still stretched above her head, his body filling hers and then retreating, only to pump back into her deeply. Within seconds, she was matching his tempo. Both of their movements were wild and a bit desperate. He dropped her wrists and she looped her arms around his neck. He cradled the back of her head as he drove into her, incited by the way she dug her fingers into his skin, scouring his flesh.

"Oh fuck," he said, his mouth pressed against her throat. "Alana, I can't . . ."

She tensed around him, every nerve pulsing and flaring as he pounded into her. No doubt her backside would be a bit bruised come tomorrow, but her hoarse cry of release said it all. She wasn't going to be upset by having to carefully sit down. He quickly followed, fusing their bodies together. She latched onto him, panting and experiencing the aftershocks as his chest rose against her swiftly.

"Alana," he breathed, voice ragged.

She dropped her head to his warm shoulder, squeezing her eyes against the rush of hot tears. Her arms trembled, but it seemed to have very little to do with what they'd just done, and more with the fact that after today, it would be the last time. It had to be before it was too late.

But an evil little voice whispered that it was already too late.

Chapter Seventeen

Alana was running.

Chandler was a lot of things, but he wasn't fucking stupid. And he'd meant what he'd said. Kind of. He'd let her have the facade of running, because she wasn't going to get far.

He knew that the woman felt the same way he did. She may not be able to say the words, but it was everything else she did. Right now, she was like a cornered animal. There were only two options for her: fight it out or run.

She was going to run.

He'd kept her busy the rest of the day Sunday, not giving her much time to put whatever cockamamie plan in place, but he woke when she crept out of his bed at dawn, too early for her just to be getting ready for work.

Too bad he didn't have another excuse to keep her home. *Home.*

Somewhere over the past days, his house had become their home. A smile pulled at his lips in spite of the fact that he knew she was packing up her clothing and personal items in the room next door. Was she going to tell him? Try to sneak the bags past him? Curiosity filled him, making it hard for him to remain in bed and see this through.

If he tried to stop her, it would only make her resist harder, but it wasn't like he was going to let her buzz around the city without his protection. With anyone else, he wouldn't let the person out of his sight if he were the one doing the job, but this situation was different. Feelings were involved and all that shit, which was why getting involved with a client was a big no-no, but he'd taken care of that, too. Murray was parked down the street, waiting just in case she called a cab.

Damn Chad and his mouth. He wanted to greet his brother with his fist to the face again, but he knew that even if Chad hadn't shown up and made an ass out of himself, this was inevitable. Something would've triggered her if it hadn't been her deepening feelings. He wasn't a psychologist, but it didn't take one to see that her commitment issues were obviously attached to her mom and he wasn't sure exactly how he would overcome something like that.

But he would.

Chandler didn't ever give up.

Her soft footfalls hurried down the hall and he stilled, his eyes drifting toward the closed bedroom door. He needed to be tied down, because lying there was probably the hardest thing he'd ever done.

Just when he thought she was going to leave, he heard her outside his door again. Closing his eyes, he forced his breathing to move slowly. The door cracked open and he felt Alana creeping in, moving quietly to the side of the bed he was "sleeping" on. The lovely scent of vanilla and lilac teased his senses and his cock immediately swelled, more than ready to get a little physical.

Her soft lips brushed his cheek and she whispered, "Good-bye."

And then she was gone.

Chandler forced himself to stay in the bed until he heard his front door close and the silent beep of the alarm resetting. Throwing off the sheet, he looked over at the nightstand. Beside his cell was a folded piece of paper. His eyes narrowed as he picked it up, already knowing what it was before he scanned the handwritten note.

It even started off with *Dear Chandler*.

He snorted.

Things have been fun. Blah. Blah. *Time for this to end.* Blah. Blah. She would find another security firm. Email her the cost of his services? What the fuck? Did she really think he was going to charge her for any of this? She even left her email address.

Her fucking email address.

That was the only thing that pissed him off.

Picking up the phone, he called Murray. He answered on the first ring. "She's in the rental car. I'm following her now."

"Perfect. Let me know where she ends up," Chandler said, crumpling up the Dear John letter. "And I'll take over from there."

Alana felt like a different person sitting behind her desk at work. Get Well Soon flowers adorned her office. The roses from the creep must've been removed, because they were absent. She hadn't reserved a hotel room yet and there was a list of security firms she knew of in the city she planned on calling once work calmed down.

She had no idea how much Chandler would charge for his services so far, and God knew he would after her bitchtastic exit this morning. A letter? She had actually left him a letter? And she would need to check into another hotel, but maybe none of that was necessary. Out of the mail that one of Chandler's employees had picked up for her, there hadn't been any suspicious letters. Maybe this guy had moved on or gotten hit by a car or something?

And it was time that she moved on.

In reality, she wasn't the same woman who had stared at her schedule last Monday. More so than the physical changes—hair down, wearing a white blouse and linen pants and no suit. Admittedly, she was a hell of a lot more comfortable dressed as she was, but there was an ache in her breast that had started the moment she walked out of Chandler's house and had only grown over the last couple of hours.

Had she done the right thing by leaving Chandler this morning? It had to be. What he said in the shower the day before had to be the lust talking and nothing more. Besides, leaving him now was like ripping a Band-Aid off a wound—rather it be quick and a bit painful than drawn-out and destructive.

No matter what, she wouldn't end up like her mom.

But as she attended the weekly meeting with the publicists, chatted with Ruby, and fielded a hundred comments about being shot and all that drama, she felt like she was . . . She was *faking* it all. It was the best way she could describe how she felt. As if she were doing nothing but lying to herself and others, telling them and herself that she was okay. That everything was fine. But it wasn't. Not really. Her skin was stretched too tight, as if she were wearing jeans that no longer fit after gorging on a meal.

Sipping her lukewarm coffee, she pushed thoughts of Chandler and her own question out of her mind and concentrated on work. For a while, it worked like it always had. She turned off her cell phone, because she really didn't think she could deal with it if Chandler contacted her, and threw herself into the phone calls with reporters, checked in on the senator, and scheduled an "impromptu" photo shoot of him reading to kids at the local Boys and Girls club. She worked through lunch and answered emails well into the late afternoon.

It was only when the office had quieted around her, blinds had been drawn, and Ruby had left for the day, that she powered off her computer. As she started to stand, she glanced over at the window. With the fading sun pushing through the thin slats in the blinds, she watched the tiny specks of dust floating in the streams of light. That was how she felt, simply floating.

Pressure clamped down on her chest and she quickly shook her head. She had been doing so well. Now wasn't the time to break down.

She placed her purse on the desk when the door to her office opened. Turning, she expected to see a lingering coworker come through the door, but what she saw stopped her dead in her tracks.

"Steven?"

Chandler was hanging around outside Alana's firm, obsessively watching. It was well beyond the time that she should've left work, but she hadn't stepped foot outside. There was a back entrance to the office building, but it was butted up against an alley, and the parking garage exited out onto the street. And her rental car was still in the garage. He had checked twice now.

Impatient, he pushed off the wall and slipped into the bottom floor of the garage. The fact that there wasn't any security monitoring the comings and goings after five p.m. grated on his nerves.

He beat feet to the third floor, spying the tan sedan by itself. She was still here.

Chandler stopped in the middle of the parking garage, torn between wanting to bum-rush her office and waiting for her out here. He knew that she wasn't going to be happy to see him, but both of them were going to have to put their emotions aside. There was no way he was going to allow some other crackpot security firm to step in and protect her.

He waited another good ten minutes before his patience had reached its limit and he started toward the entrance door. One way or another, he was going in there, getting his woman, and bringing her home, where she was safe.

Steven didn't look like the last time she'd seen him. Gone was the perfectly coifed hair and clean-shaven face. His glasses sat crooked on the edge of his nose, and the lenses appeared dirty, as if he hadn't wiped them in days. His shirt was buttoned unevenly and clung to his wiry frame

Concern filled her as she studied him. "Is everything okay, Steven?"

"Where in the hell have you been?" The door shut behind him, slamming like a crack of thunder, causing her to jump. "Answer me!"

She blinked slowly, her hands following to her sides. "I . . . I don't understand."

He stopped in front of her desk, his face flushed. "Where have you been!" he shouted, and Alana jumped once more, shocked. "You haven't been at your apartment. You haven't been at work. Where have you been!"

Oh my God . . .

Instinct flared alive and she took a step back. At first she had thought something terrible happened to him. Perhaps a death in the family, but now . . . oh no, her thoughts were going to a terrible, dark place.

"Did you forget about calling me?" he mocked, advancing on her. "But that's right. You had no intention of doing that."

"I thought . . ." She swallowed hard. "You're engaged."

Steven laughed, and the sound was unnaturally harsh. "I'm not engaged. There's no one else. No one but you."

Icy fear balled in Alana's chest, a kind of terror she had never felt before. It slithered through her veins, turning her blood to slush and freezing her where she stood. Her brain hadn't caught up with what was happening. It absolutely refused to believe that Steven had been the person responsible for the letters, the vandalism to her car and apartment, and now he was here, alone with her.

The tiny hairs on the back of her neck rose as her gaze darted toward the door. Could she make it? She was sure as hell going to try.

"You ruined everything," he seethed, walking around the desk. "And you had no idea!"

She took a step back, bumping into her office chair. "I'm sorry, Steven, but I don't—"

He moved so quickly, she didn't have a chance. Or maybe she was so unprepared for what was happening that she just didn't react accordingly. His fist snapped out, catching her on the jaw.

Pain burst along the side of her face and she stumbled to the side, banging into her desk. Lights crowded her vision and for a second, pain became everything, shooting down her neck, causing her pulse to spike rapidly.

He reached down, grabbing a handful of her hair and yanking her off the desk. A fierce burn shot over her scalp as he hauled her around the desk, dragging her.

"I loved you and you left me," he said, his fist tightening in her hair, causing her to yelp. "And I didn't mean a damn thing to you. You just up and dropped me, like I was nothing."

Her mind was reeling as she tried to break his grasp on her hair. Her foot slipped out of her shoe, throwing her balance off. She honestly didn't give two shits what his reasoning was at this moment. All she wanted was to be free and out of this office. Spying the heavy hole puncher on her desk, she reached for it, but Steven jerked her head back.

With a wide swipe of his arm, he knocked the puncher off the corner of her desk, along with the container that held her pens. They fell to the floor, rolling across the carpet.

"You didn't even think about me, did you? My entire life fell apart, and you just went on with your own. That's not fair." Steven reached behind him with his free hand. "I didn't even cross your thoughts. Not once?"

"No," she gasped, her fingers digging into his hand. "I didn't think about you once."

"Well, guess what?" he demanded, brandishing a knife. "No one is going to think about you ever again."

Alana eyed the wide knife, her heart sinking as a scream built in her throat. In an instant, she realized she was going to die.

Halfway across Alana's office floor, he heard the heavy thud. Instinct roared to life and he took off, racing toward her closed door.

Alana screamed.

The sound pierced him straight through the chest. He reached the door, finding it locked, and he cursed. "Alana!"

There was another scream but it was cut short by the sound of something crashing to the floor. A male's voice from inside the room exploded. How did someone get in here? The back entrance was the only way. But none of that mattered right now.

Panic punched through his gut as he backed up and lurched forward, slamming his shoulder into the door. The hinges groaned but did not give. He reared back and planted his booted foot near the center of the door, between the hinges. The door gave, snapping the lock and swinging open.

A vase of flowers and a computer screen were shattered on the floor. Among the destroyed glass and plastic, Alana struggled with a man. He had ahold of the back of her neck. An angry red bruise blossomed across her cheek, but Chandler's gaze trained in on the knife the man held in his hand, high above his head, the deadly edge fixed on Alana.

Rage shot through him like a wrecking ball and his response was cold and quick. He shot forward, clamping a hand down on the man's shoulder, jerking him.

Alana's assailant whirled, brandishing the knife and swinging in a high arc. Instinct kicked in and Chandler dipped under the man's wide, sweeping stab and sprang up behind him. The guy spun, and Chandler caught his arm. Drawing up his knee, he planted his foot in the man's stomach, sending him flying back. The assailant went down, cracking his head off the corner of the desk, and that was it. Lights out.

"Oh my God," Alana said, pressing her hand to her cheek as she lifted her wide gaze. "Oh my God, Chandler, it was him. I didn't think it was someone like him."

She took another step to the side and stumbled. Rushing to her, he caught her around the waist and turned so she didn't have to see the man. It was a good thing for the guy that Chandler didn't have his gun with him, because he would've shot and he would've shot to kill.

"I didn't know," she said in a shaky voice, and kept repeating. "I didn't want it to be him. He said . . . he said he was engaged. It was a lie. I don't . . ."

"Shh. It's going to be okay." Chandler tucked her head under his chin, against his chest. The way her shoulders moved even though she wasn't making a sound killed him. He smoothed his hand up her spine, thrusting his hand deep in her hair. "Everything is going to be okay now."

Chapter Eighteen

Everything should be okay.

Her apartment had been virtually restored. The rental insurance had kicked in and the new furniture had arrived. The fridge was stocked with fresh food, and several shopping bags were in her bedroom, ready to be emptied of her recently purchased items.

The days that followed Steven's attack blurred together. Between the police and the hospital visit Chandler had insisted on, the first twenty-four hours afterward had been full of questions and little answers.

She'd learned that Steven had lost his job shortly after she'd broken up with him due to performance issues and a looming malpractice suit. Alana hadn't had a clue, not even when she saw him the other week at the coffee shop. The police believed that Steven had somehow twisted up the end of their relationship with the loss of his job and had become obsessed with her.

Part of her was still shocked that she had so badly misjudged him, her clients, and practically everyone in the world. Never once had it occurred to her that it could be someone like him, and the idea that Steven had been so angered by her rejection all that time ago still befuddled her.

The man had been sick.

Alana roamed from one room to the next, vaguely aware of what she was doing. It was going to take a long time for her to forget the crazed look in Steven's eyes, how close the knife had come to her flesh. Staring death in the eyes like that wasn't something she ever wanted to repeat again.

If it hadn't been for Chandler, she would be dead now.

At the thought of his name, knots formed in her belly. She hadn't seen him since she left the hospital, but he would be here any second. He'd called, wanting to speak to her, and she'd agreed. She wasn't sure why. She wasn't ready to talk to him, to have the conversation they needed to.

After what happened with Steven, she was convinced that getting into any relationship was a bad idea. Her mother was crazy and Alana must bring out the crazy in other people, which probably explained Chandler's attraction to her.

She laughed at that, but the sound was harsh. Smoothing her hands down her jeans, she went into the living room and sat on the edge of the couch, her spine rigid, and she waited.

Thirty minutes later, there was a knock on her door, and her heart jumped out of her chest, landing on the carpet and doing a little jig.

"You can do this," she whispered, standing. It occurred to her as she went to the door that if she were about to do the right thing, why did she need to convince herself of that?

Chandler caused her breath to hitch in her throat as he

stepped inside her apartment. His hair was pulled back, showing off the planes of his cheekbones and the strong curve of his chin.

"How are you feeling?" he asked.

She forced a weak smile. "I'm feeling okay. You?"

"Better now." He reached out, his fingers going for the bruise on her jaw, but she stepped aside, avoiding his touch. He frowned. "Your jaw bothering you?"

"I barely feel it." That was kind of true. Every so often, if she wasn't careful, it would ache. She headed into the living room, needing to move from the close space of her entryway. "Um, would you like something to drink?"

The frown on Chandler's face deepened as he sat on the couch. "No. Come sit with me."

She hesitated, but the look that appeared on his face told her that if she didn't, he would be likely to pick her up and drop her ass on it. So she sat . . . on the farthest cushion. "It was nice of you to stop by," she said after a stretch of silence. "But as you can see, I'm doing okay."

His brows rose. "Nice of me to stop by?"

Nodding, she ran her palms over her bent knees and focused on the window. "Can you let me know how much I owe you for your services? I imagine the cost to repair my Lexus was pricey, but like I said, I do have money—"

"Are you fucking serious?" Chandler exploded.

She jumped, her gaze swinging toward him sharply. "I'm not sure I follow that question."

"You're not?" Fury darkened his eyes to a deep, midnight blue. "I didn't come here to give you a bill. It's not like I'm going to charge you."

Her lips parted. "I have to pay you. I owe you money for the Lexus, for your services—"

"Services?" He spat out the word, a muscle ticking in his jaw. "I helped you because I wanted to, Alana. I never once told you that I was going to charge you for any of this."

She stared at him, her heart thumping heavily. "Why would you do this for free?"

Chandler shook his head as he stood. "You know, this is kind of insulting. Why would I? Is it that hard for you to imagine?"

Apparently so.

He cursed under his breath. "I *care* about you. That's the reason I helped you. It doesn't have to do with anything else. And the reason I'm here now is because I care about you."

Those words formed on the tip of her tongue—those three words—but she couldn't speak them. All she could think of was her mother saying those words about every man she crossed paths with and those words leaving a trail of destruction in their path. Part of her knew that was stupid, but she couldn't get past it.

Chandler stared down at her. "You care about me. Hell, I'd wager good money that you're in love with me."

She gasped. "That's not—"

"You're a shitty liar, Alana. You took a bullet for me."

"I wasn't thinking. I didn't—"

"Bullshit. I've told you that before, and I still mean it. After everything that has happened, you can't admit to what you're feeling? You're still willing to hide behind old fears?" he demanded, hitting old wounds with an accuracy that was startling. "You're not your mother and I'm not some random guy who's going to change you or break your heart. You're a goddamn grown woman, Alana, who isn't afraid to stand up to anyone, but you're terrified of yourself."

Anger flashed through her, warring for first place with the unease building. His words . . .

"You're a lot of things, Alana. You're beautiful and stubborn as hell. You're smart and determined. You're damn good at your job," he said, holding her stare. "But you're a coward. And you'd better wake up before the best damn thing walks out of your life and you do end up just like your mother."

Stunned by what he said, all she could do was sit there, and when she didn't say anything, Chandler cursed under his breath again. "I've told you that I don't mind the chase, and I have no fucking problem chasing after you, but I refuse to run after a ghost. And that's what you are if you can't let go of your past with your mom. I won't chase a ghost."

Then he spun, his long legs quickly eating up the distance between her and the door. And then . . . then he was gone, the door slamming shut behind him.

The moment Chandler left, she knew, without a doubt, that she had made the biggest mistake of her life. It was right there, smacking her face.

Everything he had said was right.

She was a coward.

And the best damn thing to ever happen to her had just walked out the door.

* * *

239

Her heart was like a hummingbird in her chest by the time she climbed out of her newly returned Lexus and stared up at Chandler's house.

A thousand things could go wrong with this. He might not be home. He could be and he could have company—his brothers or anyone, really. He could also slam the door in her face.

Alana's stomach dipped like she was on a roller coaster of horror, but she would not run. She was *done* running and that was why she was here.

She would've come last night, but she figured he needed the time to calm down and she needed to get her head on straight. After two pints of ice cream and a good old ugly cry, she'd passed out and woke up this morning determined. She had been wrong and she wasn't going to run from what she felt any longer.

Please God, do not let this be a huge mistake.

She headed up the paved walkway, passing the sweet scented early summer flowers. On the front porch, the furniture was pristine yet inviting. Gathering up her courage, she lifted her hand to knock, but the front door whipped open before she could knock.

It wasn't Chandler who answered the door.

Chad stood there, eyebrows raised. Their eyes met, and she was struck by how similar they were to Chandler's.

"Miss Gore . . ." Chad stepped back, head tilted. "You look like you . . . want to punch someone in the nuts."

The tips of her ears burned. Did she always walk around looking like she wanted to castrate men?

"Since we really haven't chatted in a while, I know—Well,

shit, I'm hoping my balls are safe," he continued on, like he always did. "But I still feel like I need to cup myself."

Alana squeezed her eyes shut and took a deep breath. After a second, she stepped inside the door and forced herself to meet the youngest Gamble brother's eyes. "I owe you an apology."

Chad opened his mouth, but whatever he was about to say died on his lips. "Come again?"

"An apology," she gritted out. "You have every right to not like me. Not because of the things I've said to you or how I managed your case. You were a walking and partying erection six days out of the week."

His eyes narrowed.

"You needed my help. I hope ... I hope one day you come to see that." The back of her throat burned, and she felt the ugly hot rush of tears building. "But what I did to Bridget was wrong. I shouldn't have blackmailed her, and I shouldn't have made her feel like she was scum or anything. She's a really nice woman, and how I treated her was wrong. So I'm sorry."

Now, Chad just stared at her like she'd ripped off her jacket and shaken her breasts in his face.

The rush of emotion was reaching her eyes and her lower lip trembled as she struggled to keep it together. "I know you've never really forgiven me for that. I don't expect you to, and that's probably a good reason why this is really pointless—doing anything with Chandler." And now she was rambling. Great. But she couldn't stop. "I mean, you don't like me. Neither does Bridget, and I'm sure Chase doesn't think very highly of me."

"I've never said that," came a voice from behind Chad.

Chad turned, and Alana saw Chase lounging just outside the entryway to the living room. How long had he been standing there?

"I've never said I didn't like you," he said again, his head cocked to the side in the same manner as Chad. "I really don't know you, and what I do know, well—"

"It's not good. I know that." Her heart hammered as the words formed on her lips. "But I—"

"Really do look like you want to kick someone in the balls," Chase said, one eyebrow raising. "If you want to kick Chad, I'm not going to stop you."

"What?" Chad looked at his brother, scowling. "What the fuck, man? I'd like my balls to be in good working condition later."

"I don't want to kick anyone in the balls!" she shouted.

"That's good to know," came the voice she wanted to hear, she needed to hear.

Chandler filled the doorway to the living room, the gray shirt he wore stretching over his broad shoulders. Upon seeing him, she was momentarily stunned into silence and forgot both of his brothers were there. His dark hair was pulled back from his face in a short ponytail, his face freshly shaven, and his eyes were the color of the skies during a bright summer day. His expression was absolutely unreadable as he stared back at her with searing intensity.

His gaze dropped, drifting over her before returning to her face. "I thought you got rid of those horrible suits?"

Her cheeks flushed. "I did, but . . ."

He waited.

Alana couldn't bring herself to vocalize why she had dressed in the only boxy, unattractive suit she had left, especially not in front of his damn brothers. What had seemed like a good idea when she got ready this morning now felt foolish.

All of them waited—the three brothers. Seeing them together was somewhat awe-inspiring and none of them looked like they were moving from the hall.

She shifted her weight from one foot to the other. "I was wondering if we could talk? If not, then maybe later, or—" Her lashes lifted and she met his stare again. The set of his hard jaw told her it was do-or-die time. Either keep running or act like a grown, somewhat sensible adult. "I was wrong about you—about us, and you were right. I am scared. I *was* scared that I would end up like my mother and that—that was so stupid, because I'm not her and you're not any number of those guys. And I know I might've screwed this up, but I wanted you to know that I'm sorry and that I was wrong."

Chandler cocked his head to the side, just like his brothers had been, but they were all now staring at her as the silence stretched out between them. "I know," he finally said.

Out of everything she'd expected him to say, that wasn't it, and that was sort of funny, because it came as no surprise that he would be that cocky. But "I know" after making such an impassioned admission? What the hell was she supposed to do with "I know"?

She stared at him as a slow, one-sided grin appeared on his lips. Her brows pinched. "Is that all you're going to say?"

"No."

Alana waited . . . and waited.

Chad and Chase waited, looking like they needed a big bowl of popcorn.

"I was angry and frustrated," he said, unfolding his arms, his eyes holding hers as he walked forward. "I left your place last night, Alana, but I didn't leave you."

I didn't leave you.

Her breath caught as the four words sunk in and when they did, there was a swelling in her chest that she was sure could've taken her straight up to the ceiling.

"So, you see, I've been waiting for you." He stepped closer, so close that their legs brushed. "I was going to give you till this evening to come to your senses and then I was going to come after you."

"You were?"

He nodded. "Remember? I told you that I like to chase."

She remembered.

"And you know what I like better than the chase? The capture," he said, cupping her cheek. "I enjoy the capture the most."

Her pulse pounded in several places throughout her body. "Why doesn't that surprise me?"

Chandler smiled as he smoothed his thumb over her cheek. "Is there something you want to say to me?"

Sweet relief eased the taut muscles in her neck and happiness bubbled up inside her. She swallowed against the sudden knot in her throat. "This was easier than I thought it was going to be?"

He laughed, dropping his forehead to hers. "I was thinking you wanted to tell me something else."

She reached up, spreading her palm against his cheek. The words were surprisingly easier to say than she could've ever imagined. "I love you."

His eyes fell shut as he sucked in a deep breath. "I'm glad we don't need another near-death experience for you to admit that."

"Me, too," she whispered, stretching up and kissing him softly. "Don't you have something you want to say?"

"Remember my fantasy?" His lashes lifted. Heat shaded his eyes into the blue of lapis lazuli. "About the first time I saw you?"

Someone, maybe Chase, cleared his throat behind them, but it went largely ignored.

That wasn't what she was looking for, but she would go with this. "Yes. I remember."

"And look at you. Your hair pulled back, wearing one of those god-awful suits. I think you did that on purpose."

A smile teased her lips. "I might have."

"Hmm," he murmured as he reached around, gently unwrapping the bun and letting her hair fall down her back. "And why did you do that?"

"I thought it might help my case."

He took her hand and pressed it to his groin. "It's helped something."

Her womb clenched. Hot, tight shudders racked her body. "I can see."

Chandler dipped his head, brushing his lips over hers. She opened her mouth, inviting him in as she clasped her arms loosely behind his neck. With that, his kiss became urgent, deepening. Nothing could've prepared her for the raw intensity of his kiss. Her senses overloaded as his tongue slipped over her tongue.

"All right, you two have an audience. Seriously," said Chad. "And I think I'm going to be scarred for life."

"Hell," muttered Chase.

"There's the door," Chandler said, never taking his eyes off Alana's. "I suggest both of you make use of it and close it behind you, or you're about to get an eyeful."

"I don't know about you," Chase said to his younger brother. "But that is not something I want to see."

"Or hear."

Alana's cheeks were burning, but so was the blood in her veins. The longer Chandler stared at her, the more she knew how badly he wanted her.

Chase was first to leave, standing in the door as he waited for his brother. As Chad walked by them, he stopped and leaned over. Whispering in Alana's ear, he said something she'd never imagined him speaking.

"Thank you," he said.

Alana sucked in a sharp breath and then the door closed behind the brothers. She would think about those two words later, let them sink in, savor them, but right now she was focused only on Chandler.

Only him.

"You don't plan on wearing this suit again, do you?" he asked, voice husky.

Her stomach fluttered. "No. Never again."

"Good. Because it's not going to be in one piece in a few seconds."

She could barely breathe, let alone think as he pulled

the suit off her shoulders, tossing it aside. He paused, pressed a kiss to the bruise on her jaw, a tender move that caused her heart to skip in her chest. Then he fisted his hands in the front of her blouse and yanked it. At the sound of the material ripping, her body flushed hot. Her shoes and pants followed quickly and within seconds, she was standing in his foyer, dressed only in her bra and panties.

Chandler stepped back, his gaze soaking her up, and then he hooked his fingers into her panties, pulling them down. Her bra came next. In his haste, he broke the fragile clasp. She didn't care. She wanted him, only him.

And she wasn't just going to stand by.

She got her hands under the hem of his shirt and tugged it off, then her fingers went to the button on his jeans. With his help, she pulled them and his boxer briefs off. His erection pressed against her belly as he backed her up against the door, fitting his body against hers.

She'd never look at this door the same again. No way.

"Tell me again," he murmured against her cheek, slipping his hand between her thighs, cupping her intimately. "Just say those three little words for me again."

"What words?" Her hips surged forward, grinding against his thigh and his hand. Pleasure spiked, making her dizzy and breathless.

Chandler growled low in his throat as he grabbed her hip, stilling her movements. "You know exactly what I want to hear you say again."

Kissing the underside of his jaw, she moved restlessly against him. She wanted to drown in him. "I love you."

247

"That's my girl." He wore a wicked grin as his thumb smoothed over her clit.

She reached down to return the favor, but he started to kiss down her throat, making a slow descent. His hair tickled her breasts as he drifted between them, and a soft sound caught in her throat as his tongue laved over the tips of her breasts and then down below, circling her navel.

Chandler knelt before her, spreading her legs wide. Lust slammed into her as he grasped her hips. His tongue glided from her navel to just above the bundle of nerves. He kissed her inner thigh, nuzzling the slick crease. The air left her lungs, and then he sliced her open with his tongue. He captured her flesh with his mouth, parting her lips with firm, determined strokes of his tongue. She cried out as he sucked at her.

Lost in the raw sensations, she grasped his hair and rocked her hips against his mouth. He growled in pleasure, dipping his tongue in and out. Her back arched, heart pounded. His tongue worked her until she was thrusting unabashedly, panting heavily. The intensity built until her body liquefied as he moved on to her clit and added a finger. His sucking and thrusting matched the tempo of her hips. She bucked and climaxed with such force that her knees went weak. He caught her, keeping his mouth on her, soaking up every last drop while her body spasmed with sweet aftershocks.

And then he stood up, grasping her hips as he lifted, and entered her deeply. He didn't move, just remained there as her body dampened his. Then he slowly withdrew, eliciting a whimper from her.

"You know what I want." His voice was dark and rich with seduction.

Alana didn't know until he had her on her hands and knees on the foyer floor and he'd knelt behind her. His hand curved over her bottom and she clenched up, expecting a sharp slap. Instead, he slipped a finger into her and then pulled out. A wicked thrill trilled through her blood.

"Yes," she moaned, rocking back, gasping as the pressure increased.

"Good God, woman, you're going to kill me."

Then she felt his erection replacing his fingers. Her muscles tensed with anticipation. She knew this would be rough. It would be raw. It would be what she wanted.

"God," he said, voice guttural. He smoothed a hand down her spine and then grasped her hips. "Tell me how badly you want this." When she didn't respond, his hand moved back up her spine, his fingers wrapping around the edges of her hair. He tugged hard enough to send a wave of prickles across her skull and another shudder deep inside her. "Tell me, Alana."

"Yes."

The tug came again, and she cried out, already so close. "Yes, what?"

"Yes," she gasped. "I want this badly. I want it more than anything."

"That's my girl." One hand moved to the junction of her thighs. His fingers caught the throbbing bundle of nerves and he played there. Pleasure radiated out from her core, mixing with the sharp bite of pain. The sensation was heady, thoroughly sensual.

Once he was in, he shuddered as he wrapped his other arm under her breasts, holding her in place. When he started to move in slow and steady strokes, she thought she'd die from the pleasure, from the downright wickedness of what they were doing in the middle of his foyer, in broad daylight.

"You're mine now," he murmured against the flushed skin of her back. "Completely mine."

It was true. She couldn't deny it. She was *his*. And he was *hers*.

A sharp swirl of tingles rushed through her body. Behind her, he moved his powerful body at a faster rhythm. Her hands slid over the tile.

"I love you, Alana," he said, voice thick with emotion. "I love you."

Lightning flew through her veins. The orgasm came fast and hard, absolutely mind-blowing in its intensity. Her cry mixed with his as he let go. His hips pumped, throwing her headfirst into another orgasm. He stayed against her for what felt like forever, his body sealed to hers. When he did pull out, she already missed him.

Chandler turned her in his arms, kissing her cheeks, the lids of her eyes, and then her lips. Holding her close, he sat back, buck-ass naked, and pulled her into his lap.

Their eyes met.

"You never have to give away a piece of you to me," he said. "But you can have as many pieces of me as you want. You can have all of me, for forever."

Alana felt the emotion swell in her throat as she lifted her head, blindly seeking his kiss. Words didn't seem like enough, but she forced them out, meaning them. "I trust you with my pieces—all of me. I love you."

Epilogue

Bridget Rogers, soon to be Bridget Gamble, made an absolutely stunning bride. Her mane of vibrant red hair was twisted up, and soft curls fell in every direction. Pearls adorned the style, matching the beading in her gown. Wispy tendrils surrounded her face that was flushing with excitement.

Tears burned the backs of Alana's eyes. She'd never seen someone more in love or happier.

Well, that wasn't correct.

When Alana looked in the mirror every day, she saw the same glazed eyes and soft, distracted smile, and most surprisingly, it didn't scare her or make her want to run for the hills. How absolutely annoyingly stupid she had been. Being in love with a man who deserved those feelings and earned the same was truly amazing. And she was a fucking idiot for denying Chandler, but she'd rectified that quickly, and last night, and this morning, and in the car ride to the chapel . . .

Alana flushed. Thinking about sex in a church was super inappropriate.

And she loved it.

Bridget turned, her smile nervous and excited. With the cinched waist and heart-shaped bodice, her hourglass figure was perfect for the dress.

"How do I look?" she asked, fingering the single pearl necklace around her neck. "Is it too much?"

Madison Daniels shook her head. "Too much? Since when do you worry about anything being too much?"

"You look beautiful," Lissa said. Madison's brother's wife held a sleeping newborn to her chest. A towel shielded her pink bridesmaid's dress. "And the shoes? Perfect."

Bridget hitched up her dress, revealing a gnarly shade of pink platform heels. "You like?" Bridget asked Alana.

She laughed, approaching the tight-knit group of women like one would creep upon a nest of vipers. "Do you really want me to answer that?"

"Pink is not your color?" Bridget teased, letting her dress slip down.

Alana shook her head, strangely nervous. All the women had welcomed her with open arms, even Bridget, but she hadn't had a lot of close female friends and she was surprised to find herself in the back of the church with Bridget and her bridal party.

Rubbing one hand over her still-flat tummy while eyeing the slumbering baby, Maddie shook her head. A big old ring caught the light in the room, twinkling. Chandler had said he was surprised that Chase could still walk on two legs after he and Maddie broke the news to her parents. Of course they were thrilled that they'd be grandparents again, but Mr. Daniels had wanted the ring to come before the baby.

"Just think," Maddie said, smiling. "All this started at a wedding."

Lissa grinned as she patted the baby's back. "That is true. What a difference a year makes."

Bridget crossed the room, and before Alana knew what she was doing, the woman enveloped her in a strong hug. "Thank you," she said, her voice thick. "If it wasn't for you, I wouldn't be here right now."

"About to get married!" added Maddie.

A ball of emotion clogged her throat. "You really don't have to thank me, Bridget."

"Yes, I do." She pulled back, clutching Alana's shoulders. "I do have you to thank. So does Chad."

Maddie giggled. "Maybe you should become a match-maker instead."

Alana shook her head, laughing. "Oh no, I think I'll stick with perverted politicians and whiny celebrities."

"Well, that does sound more interesting." Lissa shifted the small bundle in her arms as the door opened and Chase popped his head in, grinning. "We have company."

"We're about ten minutes from start and Chad looks like he's about to pass out. Just thought—"

"What?" gasped Bridget, eyes widening.

Mrs. Daniels shoved Chase aside, entering the room as she straightened the corsage on the chest of her dress. "Chad isn't about to pass out, dear. If anything, he's just having a hard time waiting. He wants to see his bride and we all know how impatient Chad is."

Maddie sent Chase a dark look. "That wasn't nice."

Chase looked completely unrepentant as he winked and

slipped back into the hall. Shaking her head, Alana turned back to the woman. "Well, I'm going to head out. Bridget, you seriously look beautiful."

"Thank you," she replied, but her eyes were unfocused, and Alana knew she was already out there, walking down the aisle.

Saying her good-byes, Alana headed for the door, but Mrs. Daniels stopped her. "Alana, dear, don't forget we saved you a seat with the family. So don't sneak off to the back."

Her cheeks flushed and she nodded, murmuring her thanks. Not only had the Gambles accepted her, but so had the Daniels clan. For the first time, Alana had a family—a big, extended family.

"Did you see that the new gasmask came in yesterday?" Mrs. Daniels said to Maddie, smiling broadly. "Your father is planning on checking it out later. I figured either you or Mitchell would want to be the one using mace."

A slightly weird extended family.

Smiling, she slipped out of the room and into the hall, passing where Mitchell and Chase were arguing over the pros and cons of breastfeeding. Alana smiled in their direction but hurried down the hall before she caught baby fever.

She made it to the end of the hall when a door to the left opened suddenly. An arm snaked around her waist, pulling her inside the mostly empty room. Her back was pressed against a rock-hard chest and stomach. Soft hair teased her cheeks as she felt warm, firm lips press a kiss to her throat.

"You look damn sexy." Chandler's deep voice rumbled through her body. "Love the dress."

Said dress was a soft lilac, with sleeves and ending at the

knees. It was nothing special, just a plain thing and definitely not that sexy, but it only took seconds for her to realize why he found it so alluring.

Chandler slid a hand up under her dress, along her bare thigh. Easy access. Her body flushed and grew hot as her toes curled in her heels. She leaned into him, tipping her head back against his chest. He made a deep sound in his throat as he moved his hand up over her hip, his fingers toying with the delicate string of her panties.

Grabbing his arm, her fingers sank into the crisp material of his groomsman's tux. "Thank you. I haven't gotten to see you in your suit yet."

"I look awesome."

Alana laughed. "Modesty is an attractive trait."

"I've been waiting for you to come out." His hot breath blew across her cheek, and she shuddered.

A wicked thrill ran through her, tightened her nipples until they pushed against the lace and the soft material of her dress. "Chandler, seriously . . ."

"I've missed you." He kissed her neck again.

She bit back a sigh that would only further provoke him. "I think only forty-five minutes have passed since we were last together."

"That doesn't matter." He slipped his hand up, cupping her breast through her dress. His nimble fingers found the tip of her breast, teasing her mercilessly.

Her pulse quickened. "Chandler, we are in a church, for crying out loud."

"So? I thought we were working at being more inappropriate?" he asked, moving his hand to her other breast.

Her body tensed, like a coil spiraling. "But it's a *church*."

"And that's like the height of inappropriate, isn't it?" He shifted behind her and she felt his arousal against her buttocks. He easily twisted her panties to the side as he bunched up her skirt. "Just think, what will we have left after this?"

"I'm sure you'll come up with tons of other inappropriate things." Like anal beads, butt plugs, the Cadillac of vibrators, and the good Lord only knew what else Chandler would bring into sexual play.

Her resistance to him was never anything to brag about. It was practically non-existent, especially when his tongue followed the path of his kisses along her neck.

Alana focused on the wall, thankful it didn't have a cross or a picture of Jesus on it, because that would've been super awkward. "The wedding is about to start, you perv."

"This will be a quickie. I already want to come." His hand dipped between her thighs and she gasped. "So do you."

It was true. She wanted him. Badly. "We're going to hell for this."

"But what a fun way to go, right?" He removed his hand long enough to unzip his pants and free his erection. Was he commando under his tux? Sweet Mary mother of every baby on this planet, he *was*. "Hold on, baby, this is going to be fast and rough."

Planting her hands on the walls, she kicked back her head as he entered her swiftly in one deep thrust. He gripped her hips as he pumped into her. He was so hard inside her, his pace frenzied and at the same time languid, as if they both had all the time in the world.

Tension built deep inside, stoked tighter with every steady, maddening thrust. Her back arched against him as she ground back against his hips. He grunted and pressed a hot kiss below her ear.

"I love you," he said, his pace picking up.

Her body started to convulse at those words and her mouth opened. Sensing she was about to let out an ear-piercing scream, he clamped his hand down on her mouth, silencing her. Bliss washed over her as she came, her body pulsing around his. He stiffened and quickly followed, his voice a hoarse groan in her ears. Their bodies were reluctant to calm down and part. Her heart was pounding and Chandler was still moving in her slowly, causing little after-shocks to zip through her.

There was a knock on the door and then Chase's voice booming through the walls. "Five minutes until the wedding starts, Chandler. Time to put the cock away."

Alana's face flooded with heat. "Oh my God . . ."

Chandler chuckled. "Ignore him."

"I'm going to die of embarrassment."

"No, you're not." He kissed her cheek again and then moved his hips once more, causing her to catch her breath. "Damn," he groaned after several moments passed. He eased out of her, kissing her cheek. "Now I need a nap."

"You and me both." She remained still as he tucked himself back in and then rearranged her panties and dress. Then she faced him. "I look like I just had sex, don't I."

"Maybe." Chandler laughed as her eyes widened. He

smoothed his fingers through her hair, draping the long, dark locks over her shoulders. "No. You look well-loved."

"Well-loved?" There was that swelling in her chest again, and instead of it being pesky or annoying, she wanted to float away right with it. "I like the sound of that."

"I bet you do." He kissed her, his lips lingering. "I need to go."

"I know." She stretched up on the tips of her toes, bringing their mouths together. "I love you."

He shuddered. "I'll never grow tired of hearing you admit that."

She smiled as she forced herself away. "I'll be looking for you out there."

Chandler offered her his hand, and together they left the room. Luckily the hall was empty, and they parted ways when they came upon the rest of the men. Alana walked to the front of the packed church, full of friends, family, and ball players, finding her seat and thankful that she wasn't walking funny and no one was giving her the stink eye.

Mrs. Daniels patted her knee, and she smiled at the older woman. One day, when Chandler proposed—because she knew he would—she wanted all of them at her wedding.

Chad and his best men entered, lining up beside the altar. Her gaze traveled over the men. Chad, who looked ridiculously handsome in his tux and very nervous, past Chase, who was elbowing Chad in the side, and then to Chandler, who stood next to Mr. Daniels and Mitchell.

Her gaze moved back to Chandler's.

Chandler winked.

A slow smile crept across her flushed cheeks. The bridal

song began and as the audience twisted in their seats, one after another, and Bridget made her grand, beautiful entrance and Mrs. Daniels swallowed a soft cry, Alana couldn't wait to see what other inappropriate things Chandler Gamble had in store for her.

Acknowledgments

Writing acknowledgments is never an easy thing to do. No matter what, I always feel like I'm forgetting someone. Then I feel like a giant douche canoe and things just get awkward from there on out. So I'll try my best to not let that happen. A big thanks to the team at Entangled Publishing—Liz Pelletier, Heather Howland, Heather Riccio, and Rebecca Mancini—for bringing the Gamble Brothers to life via edits, cover, publicity, and foreign rights sales. Another thank-you to my agent, Kevan Lyon, and to Stacey Morgan—always the first person to read whatever it is that I write and help do typo damage control. Thank you to KP Simmon and the team at Inkslinger.

And to the following people for helping me keep the sanity—Laura Kaye, Tiffany Snow, Lesa, Sophie Jordan, Jen Fisher, Vi (I spelled it correctly), and Damaris. You ladies rock. I think we need to come up with a cool group name or something.

Another big, squishy thank-you to bloggers, big and small. Y'all put so much time and love and money and effort into spreading your love of books. THANK YOU.

None of this would be possible without you, the reader.

There are not enough thank-yous in the world to truly translate how grateful I am when you pick up a book of mine.

OBSESSION
9781473615922

He's arrogant, domineering, and... To. Die. For.

Hunter is a ruthless killer, working for the Department of Defense. Most of the time he enjoys his job... but now he's been saddled with keeping a human from danger, and it's chafing pretty badly.

When Serena Cross witnesses her friend's murder, she's thrust into a world where her enemies would kill her to protect their otherworldly secret. Everything's topsy-turvy, and the Arum who's been sent to protect her is totally arrogant.

Hunter and Serena ignite each other's tempers even as they flee from danger – and yet, despite their differences, it seems they might be igniting one another's passion, too...

Available in ebook and paperback

HODDER

UNCHAINED

9781473615939

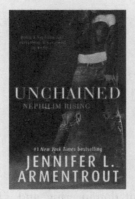

Being a Nephilim isn't everything it's cracked up to be...

Between the creatures who want demon-hunter and Nephilim Lily Marks dead and the forbidden fallen angel who just wants her, Lily is about ready to trade in forever for a comfy job in a cubicle farm.

Lily knows that getting close to mortal enemy Julian is enough to have her thrown out of the Sanctuary, the home of the Nephilim. It's career suicide, but Lily can't ignore the way he makes her feel.

Then there's the dangerous, unknown traitor working from within the Sanctuary: someone determined to frame Lily and get her kicked out. Her only hope is to discover the real traitor before she loses everything – and she'll need Julian's help. That is, if Julian is really there to help her...or destroy her.

Available in ebook and paperback

HODDER

THE RETURN
9781473611573

A year ago, Seth made a deal with the gods – and pledged his life to them. Now, Apollo has a task for Seth: one which sees him playing protector over a beautiful, feisty girl who's strictly off-limits. And for someone who has a problem with restraint, this assignment might be Seth's most challenging yet.

Josie has no idea what this crazy hot guy's deal is, but he arrives in her life just as everything she's ever known is turned upside down. Either she's going insane, or a nightmare straight out of ancient myth is heading her way.

Josie can't decide which is more dangerous: an angry Titan seeking vengeance? Or the golden-eyed, secretive Seth – and the white-hot attraction developing between them...

Available in ebook and paperback

HODDER